Mills & Boon Classics

A chance to read and collect some of the best-loved novels from Mills & Boon – the world's largest publisher of romantic fiction.

Every month, four titles by favourite Mills & Boon authors will be re-published in the *Classics* series.

A list of other titles in the *Classics* series can be found at the end of this book.

Mary Burchell

EXCEPT MY LOVE

MILLS & BOON LIMITED
LONDON · TORONTO

Australian copyright 1978
Philippine copyright 1978
This edition 1978

This edition © Mary Burchell 1978

ISBN 0 263 72899 4

Set in 10pt Monotype Plantin

Made and Printed in Great Britain by
C. Nicholls & Company Ltd
The Philips Park Press, Manchester

CHAPTER I

'THAT'S the lot, Miss Murril. The letter to Joup & Joup must go before five, with the extract from the June account. The rest will do later.'

And with a nod, but not even a glance in her direction, Oliver Leyne dismissed his secretary.

Erica went into the inner room where most of her work was done. Her employer's impersonal manner left her unperturbed nowadays, though when she had first been promoted to the dizzy heights of private secretary, his curt air had often set her wondering feverishly if she had done anything to anger him.

Not that his anger was such a brutal or shattering thing. It took the form of quiet, cold displeasure rather than any bullying outburst. But, almost from the first week, a quick impersonal word of praise from him had had the power to make her happy for the rest of the day, while his disapproval could plunge her into despair.

'He's a woman-hater, you know,' one of the other girls had stated with great positiveness when Erica had first come into the firm as a nervous new shorthand-typist.

'How do you know?' Erica had asked, with not unnatural curiosity.

'It's written all over him,' was the unanswerable reply.

Erica, a little more cautious in her own judgments, had said, 'But we only see his office manner—and not very much of that. He may be quite different at home.'

'At home!' repeated her informant with good-natured contempt. 'At home! Have you ever seen his home?'

'Well, no,' Erica had to admit that she had not. For one thing, she had not been in the town long enough to see anything much.

'Then just go and look at it one evening when you want something really bright to do. It's bad enough from the outside, but I've seen it inside, too. I had to take some

5

papers up there once when old Mr. Leyne was away with one of his heart attacks.'

'What's the matter with it? Is it shabby, do you mean?' asked Erica with little more than amused curiosity at that time.

'Shabby? Oh, no. Grand as the Hilton. You can imagine old Leyne and his son sitting in the middle of it, discussing the prospects of the iron and steel trade, and other glamorous things, and not half a smile between them.'

Erica had laughed. But even then she had thought curiously, 'It's no life for a man who looks like Oliver Leyne.'

In those days, the firm had been very much 'Leyne & Son,' with Oliver's father as undisputed head of the concern. He had built it up himself from practically nothing, and he loved every bit of it. It was said in the town that he had even built his great house where he could get up in the night if he liked and look out at the sullen glow of the furnaces burnishing the night sky. It was romance and religion and the very reason for existence to him.

He was a hard man in his way. Not, perhaps, because of any inherent cruelty in his nature, but simply in the sense that a one-idea man must be hard. He saw nothing but his own goal and ambitions. And he would have sacrificed anything and anyone to them.

Erica used to wonder sometimes what would have happened if his only son had *not* chosen to carry on the business. She felt certain the clash would have been terrible, and she could never quite decide which of the two would have proved the harder.

However, it was an unnecessary speculation because Oliver was in the business—very much a part of it. He very seldom visited the Works themselves—wandering round fascinatedly, as his father would—but he was a brilliant organiser, and the office side of the concern was almost entirely in his hands.

And then, when Erica had been on the typing staff for about a year, old Mr. Leyne was stricken down by the heart trouble which had threatened collapse more than once. It left him feeble and broken—only his passion for his great business undiminished. And in that the doctors forbade him ever to take an active part again.

There had never been very much love lost between the father and son, but perhaps Oliver understood something of the tragedy of the old man who still had the wish to go on, but no longer the power. At any rate, Erica saw, he did his utmost to be patient when his father came down, as he often did, and tried to interfere in what was now only a querulous ineffectual way.

She had every opportunity of studying the relations between them, because—most amazingly—one of Oliver's first moves had been to make her his private secretary.

Even now, when she thought of that totally unexpected— 'Will you sit down, Miss Murril? I want to speak to you about your work'—Erica felt again the uneven beating of her heart, the nervousness which had seemed to put a hand round her throat, choking back her voice almost to a whisper.

'What have I done?' she had thought distractedly. 'Have I been careless? Is he going to sack me?'

He seemed utterly unaware of her suspense, although she knew her eyes must be looking enormous, their clear grey almost lost in the black of her widening pupils.

'You have been with us, I think, just over a year, Miss Murril,' he stated in that unsmiling way of his.

'Yes. A year and six weeks.'

He had smiled faintly at that.

'I see you are accurate in this, as in everything,' he remarked.

'Then it can't be carelessness,' thought Erica, drawing a difficult breath.

'I expect you know that there will be a good many changes in the firm owing to my father's retirement,' her employer went on. 'Mr. Fearon has been a good deal more than my secretary for some while, and now he is going on to the executive staff. That leaves me, of course, without a secretary.'

Erica passed the tip of a very pink tongue over her dry lips, and waited. Her anxiety was taking on a new but delicious acuteness.

'I have watched your work for the past year, and I notice

that you are quick, conscientious and intelligent.' He spoke a little as though he were ticking off the good points of a horse, but she forgave him without difficulty. 'Above all,' he added slowly, 'I notice you are absolutely faithful. It is a rare quality. Much rarer than the other three I have mentioned.'

Erica blushed until the tears came into her eyes.

'Thank you, Mr. Leyne,' she got out at last. 'I—I only hope I deserve all you're saying.'

'I shouldn't say it otherwise,' he assured her indifferently. 'And because of it I've decided to offer you the post of my private secretary. You are young for it, I imagine. How old are you, by the way?' he added abruptly.

'Twenty-two—nearly,' Erica said, feeling that sounded slightly more responsible than twenty-one.

He frowned.

'So young? Well, I suppose it's a fault that will mend. Only I should have preferred someone of twenty-five at least.'

Erica suppressed the feeling that she ought to apologise for her age, and looked straight at him.

'I'll work very hard for you, Mr. Leyne,' she said earnestly. 'And very—faithfully.' Her voice trembled and she bit her lip sharply. She had been exceedingly moved by his tribute to her fidelity.

He had smiled then—the perfectly wonderful smile which he could very, very occasionally use.

'Very well, my child. I have every confidence in you,' he said. And he dismissed her with that little nod of his.

She felt afterwards that she must simply have stumbled from his presence, with those last incredible sentences revolving in her dazzled mind.

It was quite a while before she could bring herself even to tell any of the other girls, and then she found, to her amazement, that, although they envied her the substantial rise in salary, none of them envied her the actual position.

'Well, rather you than me, my dear,' said Carol Shawn, her special friend, who not only sat next to her in the office but also shared a little flat with her. 'You'll get no thanks

8

when everything goes right, and icy displeasure when anything goes wrong. It'll mean lots of rotten responsibility, and you won't like working in a room all by yourself, will you?'

'Oh, I shan't mind,' Erica said hastily, thinking of the little room which led out of Oliver Leyne's own office. That would be *hers* now. She would work next door to him all day, with the possibility of his coming in at any moment.

However, that possibility too seemed to have less than no attractions for the others.

'Imagine!' exclaimed Carol with horror. 'Imagine knowing that any minute of the day Mr. Leyne might walk in on you and work off a little of his temper.'

'He hasn't *got* a temper,' cried Erica indignantly.

But the others shrieked at that.

'He *has*, Erica. Frightfully chilly and quiet, but all the worse for that.'

Erica was silent. She thought of his saying, 'Very well, my child. I have every confidence in you.'

Oh, well, of course, they couldn't be expected to understand. After all, he hadn't said it to them!

And so Erica moved from the big, crowded typing room to the quiet little room which led out of Oliver Leyne's office. It was quite true that there was a terrifying amount of responsibility and a terrifying amount of work. It was quite true that it was a little lonely sometimes and that she missed the other girls. But, against that, was the happiness of working personally for her employer, saving him trouble and irritation and strain. In a word—looking after him in a thousand ways he never suspected.

Inevitably, her feeling for him changed, because the new responsibility made her grow up very quickly. When he had been nothing but a remote and magnificent person who sometimes deigned to dictate letters to her, she had felt a sort of breathless, almost schoolgirl adoration for him.

Now, it was something much deeper and quieter and stronger. No longer the slavish, illogical devotion of a romantic girl, but the quiet, protective love of someone who knew and understood him.

Nowadays, she would never have flared up and declared

9

preposterously that he had no temper. He had a temper—an abominable temper, come to that—which he kept in check with a good deal of conscious effort. But her greater knowledge of him told her that over-strained nerves and sometimes a very deep unhappiness prompted that sudden cold anger.

She suspected that it often had something to do with the faintly mysterious injury to his right hand. He always wore a glove on that hand and was abnormally sensitive and annoyed if anyone noticed the fact. Once or twice she had seen him use it, but always with a sort of clumsiness that brought a lump into her throat.

He could do nearly everything with his left hand, so that people were apt to overlook the fact that his right hand was usually either in his pocket or held behind him. And when he was introduced, he invariably bowed instead of shaking hands. But as that seemed quite in keeping with his cool, withdrawn air, people rarely noticed that either.

Only occasionally Erica detected an almost boyishly nervous anxiety that no one should notice. And it was then she used to know with queer certainty that his chilly barrier of reserve hid something else—something dear, yet disturbing, and not unmixed with a terrible capacity for suffering.

With a sudden start, Erica recalled herself now to the realisation that she had been idling in a most unusual manner. Even on a hot, lazy afternoon like this there was no time to spend reminiscing over the past. She must go down to the cashiers' department, and see about that account of Joup & Joup.

Passing through her employer's room, which was the only exit from her own office, she saw with satisfaction that he had gone out at last to a very late lunch. It always worried her a little when he neglected his meals for his work. Only, of course, she could never say so. He would probably have been haughtily astonished if he had known she presumed to take such a personal interest in him, reflected Erica with a smile as she went along the corridor.

All along this side of the building ran wide windows which looked on to the great yard dividing the office block from the Works themselves.

Erica seldom went over to the Works, but she found them oddly fascinating. She had said so once to her employer, but he had merely replied: 'Do you?' drily, without looking up.

'Don't you?' Erica had asked with sudden, irresistible curiosity.

'No. I hate them,' he had stated coldly. 'Have you finished that report yet?'

And Erica had felt that the subject was definitely closed.

She thought of that now as she went downstairs and through into the cashiers' department. Oh, well, she didn't often make the mistake of asking personal questions.

The head cashier greeted her cordially, and several of the younger men in his department raised their heads and smiled at Mr. Leyne's pretty secretary.

Her bright chestnut hair and clear grey eyes, her soft creamy skin and her red mouth, were by no means without their effect on the masculine side of the staff. And more then one of them used to wonder ruefully why it was that, even at staff dances and on other unofficial occasions, it never seemed possible to get further than the smiling courtesy with which Miss Murril treated everyone impartially.

Had they but known, the explanation was simple. 'Mr. Leyne's pretty secretary,' was a one-man girl. And the one man happened to be Mr. Leyne.

Tracing the account took a little while, and then Erica asked permission to break the rules for once and take back the ledger with her. She didn't like to be away from her office very long, and the actual checking of the account would take some time.

'Well, since it's for you, Miss Murril, I'll allow it,' the head cashier told her. 'I know I can rely on you to bring it back.'

But it was Erica's smile as well as Erica's reliability that had something to do with the permission being granted.

Back in the office once more, she set to work on the account. It was long and intricate, requiring a good deal of concentration, and she was completely immersed in her task when she suddenly became aware of the fact that her employer had returned. He was not alone, for old Mr. Leyne was with him.

Quite obviously something was wrong between them. The door was ajar, and Erica could hear the angry, complaining sentences of the old man, and the suppressed irritation in Oliver's cool, incisive answers.

She felt uncomfortable, and wished she could have made her escape, but it was impossible without passing through the room where they were.

'It's no good,' she heard Oliver say coldly. 'We've had this subject out until I'm weary of it. I have nothing fresh to say on it and—excuse my frankness—nor apparently have you.'

'You can't dismiss it like that, Oliver.' The old man's voice rose protestingly. 'You speak like some silly college boy trying to be impressive. Don't you realise that it's your whole future that's involved?'

'*My* future—yes,' came with sudden exasperation. 'For God's sake, can't you leave my future to the one person it concerns?'

Erica hastily went over and shut the door, a little ostentatiously so that they should know she was there. She knew what they were discussing now—the old man's insistence that his son should marry, and Oliver's equally obstinate determination not to do so. She had heard sharp words on the subject before, and she guessed that old Mr. Leyne tried his son's patience almost beyond endurance. But Oliver very seldom replied as violently as he had now.

This time, however, they both appeared to be too angry even to have noticed her closing of the door, and now they spoke in tones that were still perfectly audible.

'If I want to marry, I'm perfectly capable of managing the affair myself,' Oliver said in his hardest voice. 'If I don't choose to do so, I'm damned if you or anyone else shall argue me into it. It's entirely my own business.'

'It is *not*!' Erica could hear from his tone that the old man was getting dangerously excited. 'Have you no sense of responsibility? Haven't you any natural desire for someone to carry on after you're gone?'

'Oh, Father,' Oliver exclaimed wearily, 'why talk as

though we're some ancient family that must be continued at all costs? It's utterly absurd and out-of-date in any case, even if we were important.'

'I wish he would use a little tact,' thought Erica nervously, and the furious outburst from his father the next moment showed that her fears had some foundation.

'Family!—ancient family! Who cares about ancient worn-out families? Do you never think of what *we* have to pass on? One of the most splendid business concerns in the country. Why, its birth and rise have been one of the romances of the business world. And you would let it all die out with you—go to nothing! I don't understand you, Oliver. You're not like a son of mine at all.'

'I must confess I should not turn in my grave simply because this business was made into a limited liability company once I was comfortably dead,' was the cold retort.

'Limited liability——'

'Heavens, he'll have a stroke in a minute,' thought Erica, and wondered uneasily if she ought to engineer some sort of interruption.

But then the old man went on more quietly, though there was considerable anger still in his voice.

'You're utterly selfish, that's what it is. Utterly self-absorbed. You put your own ridiculous fancies and romancing before something that is a genuine duty.'

'*You* know how much I've given to this firm, and yet you can talk of my duty to it.' There was the utmost bitterness in Oliver's tone for a moment, and Erica wondered unhappily just what he meant. 'Surely, surely you can leave me some private life of my own without trying to ruin that too,' came much more quietly.

His father seemed faintly impressed. At any rate his tone changed from violence to little more than querulous protest now.

'I suppose you're still keeping up some absurd romantic notions about Dreda. Though how, after all these years——'

'That will do!' Erica heard her employer push back his chair violently. 'Dreda at least can be left out of this, and I will not—I will *not* have any more discussion.'

13

The old man started to speak again, but Oliver cut across implacably.

'I'm sorry to turn you out, Father, but I have a great deal to do yet, and absolutely no more time to waste.'

He crossed the room—Erica heard his firm, decisive tread—and evidently he held open the outer door. After a moment there was a murmur of old Mr. Leyne saying good-bye, and then the door closed, crisply and finally.

Erica knew from the sounds that her employer walked up and down his room after that, but she struggled hard to keep her mind on the all-important account.

Only when the task was complete and she began to type once more did she hear the footsteps stop abruptly. Then he came over to the door and flung it open.

'Have you been here all the time?' he asked curtly. 'Well, of course, you must have been.'

'Yes—I'm sorry, Mr. Leyne.' Erica met his dark glance as calmly as she could. 'I—I did close the door as loudly as I could,' she added apologetically.

He shot her a quick look. Then—'It doesn't matter, anyway,' he said with sudden weariness. 'Only I'm sorry you should have had the unpleasantness of a—family dispute.'

He came forward slowly and dropped into a chair by her desk. He seemed terribly dispirited, she noticed, and rather unnaturally exhausted.

'Please don't mind because of me,' she said earnestly. 'One—one has to have these discussions sometimes in any family. It was just unfortunate for you that I had to hear.'

'Discussions?' He laughed shortly. 'Is that what you call them? It's a nice polite sort of word. But they're rows, Miss Murril. Just plain, unvarnished rows. And God, I'm so sick of them!'

He put up his hand and pushed back the thick dark hair that was inclined to fall over his forehead. He was very pale, and Erica saw, with some anxiety, that his forehead was slightly damp. She scarcely knew what to think of her employer speaking so frankly. He would be sure to regret such an extraordinary lapse from his usual manner, and yet she could not leave him quite unanswered.

14

'If only Mr. Leyne didn't feel quite so warmly about it all,' she said diffidently. 'If he were to use a little more tact and reason, he might'—she hesitated—'he wouldn't alienate you as he does before he even reaches his point.'

Oliver Leyne looked up sharply, and then smiled grimly. 'Am I to understand from that that you sympathise with his cause if not exactly with his method of attack?' he asked.

'*I?*' Erica had not been thinking of her own reactions at all, and she looked astonished. 'No,' she said slowly, 'I didn't mean that. I think marrying or—or not marrying is purely a personal matter. But, as a matter of fact, I shouldn't wonder if——' She hesitated, a little appalled to find she had got so far. 'Oh, really, I beg your pardon. This isn't my business at all,' she finished hastily.

'You're quite right, it certainly is not your business. But please go on. I should like to hear your views.'

Erica coloured under the amusement in his sarcastic dark eyes.

'You wouldn't wonder if——' He prompted her remorselessly.

'If there isn't a good deal in what your father says. You probably would be a great deal happier married,' she said in a low voice.

'Really, Miss Murril? And when did you come to this interesting conclusion?'

She was unhappily silent.

'Tell me,' he commanded abruptly.

Erica wished that anything in the world would happen to stop this terrible conversation, but it was too late to turn back now, especially when he was watching her in that half mocking, half interested manner.

'Well, I've always thought you're a very lonely person,' she said a little timidly. 'It's a sort of loneliness of spirit, I mean.' His eyebrows shot up, but she went on doggedly. 'I think you have a—a great capacity for affection, but you find it very difficult to express it. People make the mistake of thinking you're unapproachable and difficult, and because you're really rather sensitive you don't know quite what to do, except live up to the character they give you.'

She didn't look at him as she finished what she was saying. It was the longest speech she had ever made to him—and certainly the most outrageous.

He leant back in his chair, and looked at her in a way that was rather hard to bear.

'Well, Miss Murril,' he said drily, 'no one could accuse you of making the mistake of finding me unapproachable. In fact, I never remember being approached in a more startling manner before.'

'I'm sorry,' Erica murmured huskily.

'Why be sorry? I told you to speak,' he said with a slightly magnificent gesture of his hand. It usually caused her some affectionate amusement when he did that sort of thing. It was so entirely unselfconscious. But just now she was too much afraid that she had annoyed him.

'You appear to have given a touching amount of thought to my personal welfare,' he remarked, not very kindly.

'Well, it's natural, isn't it, when one is working all day with someone?' Erica tried desperately to make that sound ordinary and casual.

'Is it? I should have said it was most unusual in a secretary. But I am beginning to think that my judgment may be at fault in more ways than one.'

He spoke very gravely, but Erica knew he was still finding her and the subject rather cruelly amusing.

She leant forward suddenly, her grey eyes fixed earnestly on him.

'Mr. Leyne, you think it's all very absurd, don't you?'

'A little—yes,' he admitted.

'It's not, you know.' She suddenly felt the tremendous urgency of making him listen to her. 'Will you let me ask you a question?' she said, a little breathlessly.

He inclined his head, still slightly amused.

'You're really not at all a happy sort of person, are you?' she asked boldly.

Up went his eyebrows again, and she thought at first that he was going to refuse to answer that. Then he met her eyes squarely.

'Well, then—no, I'm not,' he agreed, with a touch of something like defiance that sat oddly on him. Then he added shortly, 'But there are several reasons for that.'

'Of course.' Erica spoke again. 'There's always more than one reason for being unhappy. But nothing is so bad if there *is* someone to share things with and understand.'

'Nothing? Are you sure?' He spoke a little bitterly, and for a second she saw his glance go to his gloved hand.

'Quite sure. That's partly why Mr. Leyne feels that you would be happier married, I expect.'

'Oh, no,' Oliver laughed curtly, 'don't make any mistake about that. It isn't my happiness that is exercising *him*.' That little sarcastic glance came again, but she withstood it admirably. 'He is only concerned with what will happen to his confounded Works a hundred years from now.'

'Well then,' Erica said, 'it's why *I* am quite serious in saying that you probably ought to marry.'

He set his mouth.

'And the reason I'm quite serious in saying that I will *not* is that I can't think of any woman with whom I could bear to pass the rest of my life, or with whom I should have any expectation of finding happiness.'

Erica laughed at this sweeping assertion. And the moment she found she could laugh she felt better.

'I'm afraid the world is in a very bad way, Mr. Leyne,' she said demurely.

Her employer regarded her with a very slight smile.

'Are you by any chance presuming to find me amusing, Miss Murril?'

'Well—yes, rather,' Erica confessed.

'I don't know really why I'm not extremely annoyed with you already. But since we've got so far, we may as well complete it. Will you tell me just why you find me a figure of fun?'

'Oh, not *that*.' Erica was shocked. 'But people who make sweeping statements are always a little amusing. Before you dismiss the whole feminine population as hopeless, why don't you get to know one or two of them? Since you've given me *carte blanche* to be impertinent, Mr. Leyne—isn't the trouble with you perhaps that you don't *know* any women well?'

She caught her breath at her own daring, particularly when she saw how his face darkened.

17

'On the contrary,' he said coldly, as he got to his feet, 'I was fool enough to know one of them too well. In any case, the whole discussion is ridiculous, and I think we've wasted enough time. Please see that the urgent letters go off quickly.'

And without another word he went back into his own room, leaving Erica feeling rather shaken.

Later, when she took him the urgent letters, he read them and signed them without a word. But when she passed through his room again, on her way down to the cashiers' with the returned ledger, she knew uneasily that his eyes followed her thoughtfully right to the door.

It made her nervous about coming back to face him.

But she need not have worried. He was gone when she returned.

She heard five-thirty striking somewhere in the distance and then the familiar sounds of the office staff leaving the building. But Erica's afternoon had had so many interruptions that there was still a good deal to be done. It was not at all unusual for her to stay late in the evening. This was one of the occasions when it must be done, she decided resignedly.

Presently the door opened cautiously, and her friend Carol looked in.

'Hello, Carol. I thought you would have gone.'

'No.' Carol came forward into the room then, a debonaire blonde, gifted with unquenchable self-confidence. 'I saw your dragon going off to his lair, so I thought I'd venture in. You're not staying late *again*, are you?'

'I'm afraid so.' Erica smiled, and then sighed a little. It was hot and thundery still, and she suddenly wanted very much to go home, get into a cool frock, and laze for the rest of the evening.

'It's ridiculous,' declared Carol. 'You combine all the duties of a doormat and a machine to please that man—and what thanks do you get? Nothing at all, except "Have you finished that yet, Miss Murril? Not? You do know it's urgent, don't you?"' and Carol gave a cruelly faithful imitation of the head of the firm showing displeasure.

Erica laughed protestingly.

'Sorry, Carol. It's really my own fault this time. I wasted a good deal of time this afternoon, and I must make it up now.'

'Wasted time? My dear girl, you're unique. The person who can waste time within twenty yards of Oliver Leyne deserves a decoration.'

'Oh, go along with you.' Erica got up and came with Carol to the door. 'I must stay, really. I'll try not to be very late.'

'Roddy and I are going out to the new swimming pool, and we thought of hunting up Donald, too. Sure you won't change your mind?'

Erica glanced at her desk, and then shook her head. The swimming pool sounded almost irresistible, but the work *must* be done. Besides, if Donald came, he might choose this evening for trying once more to persuade her to marry him, and she did so hate having to hurt him by her repeated refusals.

When Carol had finally taken herself off, Erica settled down to her work in earnest. It seemed to grow hotter every minute, and thunder occasionally rolled dramatically in the distance like off-stage 'effects.'

After a while it grew so dark that she had to get up and switch on the light, and then, presently, down came the rain in hissing torrents.

'That will cool the air, anyway,' Erica thought absently, as she flicked over the pages of her notebook.

By eight o'clock everything was finished. Letters neatly piled, awaiting signature. Accounts stacked in a tray ready for posting. Erica leant back with a sigh of relief, relaxing at last. And then, immediately, her thoughts flew back to the scene that afternoon.

She hoped he wouldn't be chilly about it to-morrow, but, in any case, it was most unlike him to carry over annoyance from one day to the next. He could flare up very quickly, but he would also forget all about it with a sweet completeness that never failed to touch her.

'Anyway, he wasn't really annoyed until the end,' she told herself. And then, as the scene came back more clearly —'Of course, I should *die* if he did take my advice and

19

marry someone. I suppose I was a fool to urge him so earnestly to do the very thing that would make me utterly miserable. Only, if it really made him happy——'

She remembered his reluctant admission that he was not happy. He must have felt it pretty strongly to have put it into words.

Erica absently rolled a pencil to and fro on the desk. They said that if you really loved a man you wanted his happiness even at the expense of your own. But to have to pretend to be happy because another woman had him—that would be a cruel test to ask of anyone.

Easy enough to argue in theory—with no sign of any other woman on the horizon. 'But I wonder,' thought Erica with grim self-criticism, 'I wonder if I could live up to it.'

She got up with a sigh and took down her pale green linen coat. No good sitting brooding about things. It was more than time she went home——

And then she stopped abruptly, her hand still holding the coat.

Someone had come into the room next door.

Erica knew that she was entirely alone in the building. In the ordinary way she was not at all nervous. But this was something different. Even if she screamed, the night-watch-man's room was too far away for her to be heard——

With a tremendous effort, she went over and wrenched open the door.

'What do you think——'

Erica broke off. Oliver Leyne was standing by his desk, looking up with a slight smile from a paper he was examining.

'Oh, I—I thought——' Erica stopped. 'I've been working late,' she said rather lamely.

'So I see. You're almost too conscientious, you know. You make me selfish and apt to impose upon you.'

'Oh, no.' The rather naïve emphasis made his smile deepen, and she went on hastily, 'But why did you come back so late?'

'I haven't been home,' he said slowly. 'And I saw by your lighted window that you were still here. I've been out—

tramping.'

'Out?—in all that rain!' She put out her hand and touched his sleeve. She had never done anything so intimate before, and for a moment her finger-tips tingled with the electric thrill of contact. 'Why, you're wet through,' she said, trying to keep her face expressionless.

'Yes. It doesn't matter.'

'Oh, but it does.' She wanted to put up her hand to the damp, dark hair that was streaked back from his forehead. 'Why did you do anything so silly?' she asked gently, as though he were a naughty but very dear child.

'I wanted to think things out. You'd given me a lot to think about, you know.'

'I had?' Her eyes widened suddenly.

'Yes. You and my father between you.'

Fear clutched at her heart. What had he been working out to himself? Was it upon her, that shadowy possibility—which had seemed all right in theory, so long as it was safely in the distance?

'You mean——' she said. 'You mean——'

'Your determination that I should marry? Yes.' There was dead silence, and then he said, 'I really think it was what you said about companionship that really set me thinking. You're quite right, that is what I want. I've thought sometimes that I should go crazy with the loneliness and emptiness in that great house.' His voice dropped to an earnest, troubled undertone. 'If there were someone else there, it might not be so bad.'

Erica put her hand on his arm again.

'No, it wouldn't be anything like so bad,' she said soothingly.

He gave a little laugh at her tone, and seemed to recover from the gloom that had overwhelmed him.

'There's another thing too,' he said slowly. 'I've been realising that I was wrong when I told you there was no woman I could bear to live with always.'

Erica's heart seemed to stop altogether at that, but she forced herself to meet his eyes.

'Were—were you?' she said helplessly.

'There is one woman beside whom I *have* lived day after

day for a year now. She never irritates me nor worries me. She apparently understands my rather unpleasant nature amazingly well—even to the extent of finding me amusing at times—a very great test.' There was a second's pause, and then he said almost casually, 'Miss Murril, will you marry me?'

Erica was absolutely still.

She thought dazedly, 'The thunder has stopped and the rain has stopped and everything else has stopped.' The whole world seemed to take a deep breath and wait.

And then, before she could say anything, Oliver went on:

'Don't misunderstand me. I know quite well that you wouldn't expect to regard this as an ordinary marriage. Nor should I. There is no question of deep affection between us—nor need there be. I want—in fact, I need—your companionship, and, in return, I'm willing to give you all the—the material advantages that any wife of mine would have.'

Erica felt vaguely that she ought to reach for her shorthand notebook and take this down. It sounded so exactly like a business contract.

She heard him say, 'As you probably know, I'm a very rich man——' And then she interrupted, a little astonished at the calm and steadiness of her own voice:

'There's one thing I must know first.'

'And that is?' He, too, seemed surprised and slightly amused at her coolness.

Erica hesitated a moment longer, but she *could* not take this crazy step entirely in the dark. Yesterday she might have, but not to-day. Not with the old man's reproach about 'Dreda,' and Oliver's own bitter remark about knowing a woman too well still sounding in her ears:

She didn't look at him. She said a little huskily:

'There was someone else once, wasn't there?'

Erica felt rather than saw the suspicious, half nervous way he drew back. Then he said very stiffly:

'There was, but it was all a long while ago. Do you demand to know my whole past before you take on my future?'

'No—oh, no.' Erica was distressed at the idea. 'It wasn't

22

that at all. It was——'

'Well perhaps you have a right to know,' he interrupted. He seemed doggedly determined to tell her then. 'We were engaged. And then something—awful happened. It altered everything. I didn't know that it would alter her too. I thought she at least would be unchanged in a horribly changing world. But I was wrong. I wasn't any more use to her in the way she most wanted. So she turned me down.'

He hated saying it, Erica saw. And yet those reluctant, staccato sentences were a sort of relief, too. She was overwhelmed with pity for him, but she didn't think he wanted her pity, and so she was silent.

'She was quite cruel and callous about it,' he said, more slowly now. 'I ought to have hated her for it, but I couldn't —I can't.' He seemed entirely unaware of that extraordinary change from the past to the present.

And at that, all Erica's vague fear started into life. It was not a ghost of the past she had to fight. It was something ever-present and overwhelmingly strong.

She raised her eyes to his face, and, at what she saw there, her fear left her as suddenly as it had come. That aloofness which most people took for arrogance had gone, and in it's place was a little frown of hurt bewilderment.

'I don't know quite why she did it.' He spoke quietly, almost as though to himself. 'But perhaps I've blamed her too much.' He sighed. 'There are some things, I suppose, that a sensitive woman could not be expected to bear.'

He glanced at his gloved hand with a queer little air of resignation that was entirely foreign to him.

And then Erica knew. The tragedy of his injured hand was inextricably mixed up with an even darker shadow across his life.

She felt a burning indignation against the unknown Dreda who had been so cruel. Beautiful she might have been, fascinating she must have been, but hard, cruel and uncaring.

It was a picture that was never to leave Erica's mind entirely again. Dreda remained there as the woman who had robbed Oliver of his peace of mind, and his sense of

23

proportion.

She put out her hand now on his arm.

'I'm sorry,' she said gently. 'I'm terribly sorry. I ought not to have made you tell me.'

But at that he recovered himself immediately. His old expression returned, and he looked calm and almost hard.

'It doesn't matter now. It's all so completely past.' And she saw he almost made himself believe it at that moment. 'I could never—I *would* never—do it again. That's why I want things clear between us from the beginning.'

Erica felt her mouth go dry.

'We start with no sentimental feeling for each other'—he paused, perhaps because he saw her hand go to her throat—'and that's how it must remain. I'm well aware that most women would refuse this proposal. I'm not really hoping that you will accept it. But if you do, I promise you shall never have to complain of my generosity.'

There was a long pause—then Erica said rather faintly—'I—accept.' And then she felt that nothing could have been sillier than this Victorian reply to his preposterous proposal.

But she forgot even that the next minute, because he took her abruptly by her chin and turned up her face so that he could look at her.

'You understand—I'm offering you everything I have, except my—love. That I cannot and I will not give again to any woman.'

'I understand,' Erica said slowly. 'And I accept on those terms.'

It seemd to her that her voice came from a very long distance, and she had the odd impression it was because she had just cut her own throat.

It was Oliver's voice that recalled her finally from the mist of bewilderment and doubt. Oliver's voice saying calmly:

'Do you know that I've been keeping you here until a most ridiculous hour! Your people will wonder what's happened to you.'

'I haven't any people,' Erica told him with a smile.

'No? Do you live entirely alone?' It was odd to have him

24

look at her with that personal interest. For two years her home life had meant less than nothing to him. Now it had become part of the girl he was going to marry.

'I share a flat with one of the other girls here,' she explained.

'Which one?' He looked boyishly curious, she thought, in a way that was amusing and endearing after the cold-blooded things he had been saying.

'Carol Shawn,' Erica said.

'What, the girl with the pretty hair and nothing much under it?'

Erica laughed.

'She has very pretty hair,' she agreed demurely.

'I can't imagine you with her.' He was apparently intrigued by the problem of making their dispositions fit. 'You're not in the least alike.'

'But you don't necessarily want to spend your life with people who are like you,' Erica protested. 'Carol is a good friend and a very kind-hearted girl.'

'You mean you suffer fools gladly?' he said a little contemptuously.

'That isn't how I think of my friend at all,' Erica said with unusual sharpness.

He looked astonished for a moment at her tone. Then he cupped her chin in his hand again, but more gently this time.

'Is that meant as a reproof, my little fiancée?' he asked, smiling into her eyes.

Erica caught her breath, but she answered quite steadily: 'Yes, I think it is.'

'Then I beg your pardon, and I take back the remark about your friend.'

He was still smiling, but she thought somehow that he meant it.

'It's all right,' she said quickly. 'And let's go now.'

They went out of the building together. The sky had cleared now, and the warm night wind ruffled the curls on her forehead.

He wanted her to come and have a meal with him, but she said no, that Carol would wonder where she was.

25

'But couldn't we let her go on wondering for once? I feel that even a prosaic engagement like ours calls for some form of celebration.'

She came then, partly because it was so intriguingly sweet to have Oliver Leyne coaxing instead of commanding.

'Does he realise that he isn't quite living up to his in-human proposal?' she wondered with a hint of tender amusement. And over the intimate little meal together she watched him with an indulgence of which he was entirely unaware.

Afterwards he took her home by taxi, which seemed faintly but pleasurably extravagant to Erica. Donald and she took taxis when it was a wet night or when she was in evening dress.

When they reached her place, Oliver got out and stood on the pavement with her, looking up at the old-fashioned house which had been converted into flats.

'So that's where you live?' he said with that curiosity which sat so oddly on him.

'Yes.' Erica supposed amusedly that it was a new experience for him to be taking a personal interest in the everyday affairs of someone else. She wondered if he hoped to be asked in, but she gave no invitation. In all probability Carol was running around in her dressing-gown, scrambling eggs or washing tights.

'Good night,' she said, feeling suddenly a little awkward. 'And—and do you mind if I tell Carol about—us?'

'Of course not. Tell her if you want to. Why not?'

'I thought you might not specially want your staff to know yet that you're marrying your secretary,' Erica said simply.

'I haven't the slightest interest in the reactions of my staff to my marriage,' he assured her in his most remote manner.

'Please——' Erica felt that she didn't want them to part on that note, but she hardly knew how to put her appeal.

'What is it?'

She looked up then and smiled more pleadingly than she knew.

'Please stop being Mr. Leyne for a minute, and be Oliver instead.'

He looked extremely taken aback, and then he smiled in that fascinating way of his.

'Good night—Erica.' And he bent his head and lightly kissed her lips. 'Is that what you meant?'

It was more—so much more—than anything she had meant that Erica was absolutely wordless. Then, almost timidly, she kissed him back again, and with a murmured 'good night' she slipped away from him into the house.

There was only a short flight of stairs to the flat which she shared with Carol, but she was breathless when she reached their gaily painted green door, and let herself in.

'Is that you, Erica?' Carol called out at the sound of her key.

Carol appeared in the doorway of their tiny sitting-room.

'Snub me if I'm being inquisitive, but what *have* you been doing?'

Erica laughed.

'Oh, lots of things. I'll tell you all about it.'

She came into the room, tossed down her coat, and ruffled up her hair a little nervously.

'Well, if *that's* what overtime does for one's looks, I'm all for extending office hours,' remarked Carol.

'What do you mean?'

'Nothing. Just look at yourself in the glass, that's all. Take your time. I can curb my impatience—just.'

Erica turned slowly and stared at herself in the mirror. She felt she scarcely knew the girl who looked back at her. That was Oliver Leyne's fiancée—that girl with the wide grey eyes, and the faint pink in her cheeks. And that soft, damp mouth was scarlet against her creamy skin because he had kissed it only five minutes ago.

'Pretty, isn't she?' Carol said behind her, and Erica turned round with an excited little laugh.

'Not bad,' she admitted gaily.

'Been getting engaged?'

'Why, yes,' Erica said, a little staggered at Carol's penetration.

27

'I thought I knew the look. So that was why Donald wasn't in when we rang him up.'

'Donald? Do you suppose getting engaged to *Donald* would make me look like that? It's—it's Oliver Leyne.'

Carol shut her eyes very tightly, and then opened them again.

'Say it again.'

'I'm engaged to Oliver Leyne.'

'*The* Mr. Leyne? *Our* Mr. Leyne?'

'Of course.'

'How frightful.'

'Carol!'

'How utterly and absolutely frightful.'

'But, Carol, he's wonderful.'

'So's Mount Everest, but I shouldn't want to marry it.'

'Oh, don't be silly. He's perfectly human and lovable, really.'

'Human? Yes, that's the word. Bursting with humanity. Loves the whole world. Got that personal touch that puts everyone at their ease. You must be mad, my poor girl. Just plain crackers.'

Erica laughed exasperatedly.

'It's no good. You can't understand. But then you don't love him and I do.'

'Just so. And does he love you?'

'Why—why, yes,' stammered Erica.

'That's grand,' Carol said gloomily. 'Well, Erica, I suppose you know your own business best, but if I had to choose between marrying Oliver Leyne and jumping overboard in mid-Atlantic——'

'Yes?' Erica said anxiously.

'I'd have some swimming lessons and take a chance on the Atlantic.'

Erica came and put her arm round her friend's neck.

'Wish me luck, Carol dear, and don't be so horrid.'

Carol kissed her immediately.

'I do wish you luck, Erica—all the luck in the world. But don't ask me to be congratulatory. I think you're just about a million times too good for him.'

'Oh, no. He's a dear, really. It's only that he's been

28

unhappy so often, and——' She stopped at Carol's expression.

'All right, Erica. I'm very fond of you, but if I've got to think of your Oliver as a sensitive plant it's going to be an awful strain on our friendship.'

'I won't say any more,' Erica promised with a smile.

'Thanks. That's very generous of you,' said Carol. 'And in return I'll admit that old Carpenter the doorkeeper once told me "young Mr. Leyne" was very gay and different before he had the accident to his hand and his girl chucked him over. Oh'—she stopped abruptly—'perhaps I shouldn't have said that.'

'It's all right. I know,' Erica assured her.

'Hm. It's been quite a soul-searching evening, I take it?'

'I suppose so.' Erica smiled faintly.

'When are you going to get married?'

'I'm not quite sure. Fairly soon, I should imagine.'

'Well, don't forget it's the *girl's* privilege to fix the date. And if you must be a doormat, darling, at least don't put "please kick me" on it.'

'I'll remember,' Erica promised, and went off to her room laughing a little vexedly.

Once or twice during the next week she reluctantly recalled Carol's remark, but if Oliver still retained a good deal of his aloof, hard manner, there was something else there at times which touched her immeasurably. A sort of relaxation which seemed to surprise and please himself almost as much as it did her.

Once she found him watching her as she moved about the office.

'Do you want something?' she asked quickly.

He shook his head, and smiled a little, with his eyes still on her.

'What is it, then?'

'Nothing. I just like to watch you.'

'Oh——' Erica didn't say any more, but she treasured the incident in her own mind.

She had wondered a good deal how old Mr. Leyne would react to the engagement, and had felt distinctly nervous the first time she saw him afterwards. But although he rather

29

obviously wondered quite what his son saw in her, he appeared to be pleased with the choice.

'I'd rather he married a girl with enough sense to earn her own living than see him caught by some little nitwit with money,' he assured Erica with candour.

'Well, I'm very glad if you're pleased with his choice,' Erica said, smiling.

'Yes, I *am* pleased,' the older man told her. 'I've seen enough of you to know you're a good, sensible girl. And you're pretty, too, and healthy. You'll have nice children.'

Erica didn't know quite what she was expected to say to this, but apparently no reply was really necessary. Old Mr. Leyne always took it that people agreed with him unless they definitely made a statement to the contrary.

Well, it was going to be a little disappointing for him, Erica thought uneasily, if he ever found out just how things were between her and Oliver.

But she need not have worried, for the problem never arose. Old Mr. Leyne died in his sleep three days later, without ever seeing her again.

She was glad, when she thought it over, that it was not until after he had heard of the engagement. His son's marriage was the only thing that had exercised him greatly in the last year of his life, and he appeared to have been entirely satisfied with the arrangement made.

'Perhaps it was just as well,' thought Erica, 'that he didn't live to face the problems that arose out of it.'

In her heart, she was a little afraid of Oliver's reactions now that his father had died. It had been very largely to satisfy the old man that he had taken this extraordinary step, she remembered uneasily. Did he wish now that he had not been in quite such a hurry?

Perhaps the thought made her more serious than she knew, because one day, when she had been taking dictation from Oliver—just the same crisp, official dictation that he had always given her—he said suddenly:

'What's the matter? Are you worrying about the work, in the character of my secretary, or about something quite outside the work, in the character of my fiancée?'

Erica laughed and coloured a little.

'I'm not worrying.'

'Then why are you so serious?'

'I—I was wondering about something.'

'What?'

She moved uneasily. It was always difficult to evade his questions. She didn't answer at once, but he simply went on waiting.

'I was wondering how you felt about—about our engagement, now that your father has died.'

'In what way?'

Really, he made things very hard, she thought. She drew nervous little designs on her shorthand notebook.

'Well, it was partly to please him that you were marrying, wasn't it?'

'Oh, dear, no, it wasn't.' She had her head bent, but she could hear from his tone that he was smiling. 'I'm marrying to please myself and I assure you that my pleasure in my marriage is entirely undiminished.'

'Oh.'

'Look up, Erica.'

She glanced up at him, very slightly scared.

'All right now?' He gave her his most compelling smile.

'Oh, yes—quite all right, thank you.'

'Then will you do those letters for me, please, Miss Murril?'

She got up with a smile.

'Oh, and Miss Murril'—as she reached the door. She turned. 'Isn't it about time you resigned? You're getting married in about a month's time, I understand.'

Erica looked distressed.

'But, please, mayn't I stay on a little longer? I'd much rather.'

'Would you? Why?'

'Because I like working for you.'

He pushed back his chair abruptly and crossed the room in two strides.

'You *like* working for me? You strange child. Most people hate it. But you shall have your own way.'

She thought for a moment he was going to kiss her, but, instead, he turned away as abruptly as he had come up to

31

her. And for some reason or other she felt strangely chilled.

It was only a few days after this that old Mr. Leyne's will was published, and, for the first time, Erica realised what an immensely wealthy man her fiancé was. She thought that even he himself was rather astonished at the extent of his father's fortune, and Carol was genuinely awestricken.

'It'll take you quite a long time to spend all that,' she remarked as she hung over a newspaper, reading particulars. The papers had made the usual story of it—'From Messenger Boy to Magnate,' 'Romance of an Iron and Steel Fortune,' and so on.

One of them added that the entire fortune passed to his only son, 'whose engagement to his secretary, Miss Erica Murril, was recently announced.'

It gave Erica a peculiar feeling to see her own name in print like that. But it didn't seem to make the whole business any more real. Only Oliver's cool certainty did that —and it was a certainty that seemed to increase rather than diminish as the time drew on.

He appeared to find nothing strange now in this marriage of his, and Erica realised, with increasing warmth at her heart, that there was a new tranquillity about him, a sort of content which Carol declared to be 'the first sign that he's human after all.'

The last two weeks before the wedding seemed to fly. There was a good deal to clear up at the office, for they were to be away at least three weeks on their honeymoon in Italy. And, in addition, Erica had to leave everything in order for her successor.

To be sure, the wedding itself was to be too quiet to involve much preparation, for Erica herself had no near relations and had been only too willing to fall in with Oliver's preference for 'no fuss.'

In what seemed like another existence—before she had come as a typist to Leyne & Son—she had lived all her life in a small town in the West of England. But the death of both her parents within a few months of each other had filled the place for her with unhappy memories, and she had left it very gladly for the opportunity of a job in the famous iron works.

She had always meant to go back one day, but somehow she never had. And now she felt that, if her roots in this big manufacturing town were new, those in the place where she was born were dead.

'So really, there's nobody much you *could* ask.' Carol remarked, when they were discussing it one evening. 'Does it make you feel a bit queer not having any relations or friends of your childhood days to weep at your wedding?'

'No,' Erica said. 'I don't want anyone to weep at my wedding. And anyway, I'm quite satisfied just to have you —and Oliver, of course.'

'A very necessary part of the wedding equipment,' agreed Carol, as she got up to answer a knock at the front door.

'It's an enormous parcel for you,' she called out a moment later, and then she came into the room again with a large package.

'For me?' Erica began to struggle with the knot in the cord that tied it.

'Good heavens, cut it, girl!' begged Carol. 'You're going to be a wealthy woman in a week's time. Why bother with the minor economies now?'

'It isn't economy. It's just prolonging the excitement,' Erica assured her. 'I wonder who sent it.'

'Oliver, I suppose,' Carol said. 'At least—do you know what he's going to give you?'

'No.'

'How exactly like him to buy it without consulting you. So perfectly certain he knows best——'

'*Oh!*'

Both girls exclaimed together as the final wrappings came off, to disclose a most exquisite green suède dressing-case.

In a silence that was almost awe-stricken they examined the gold and shagreen fittings, and at last Carol sighed ecstatically, 'It's so beautiful it scarcely looks respectable.'

'Carol, don't be idiotic. But it's the most wonderful thing I ever saw. I know now why he wanted to know what colour my going-away suit was.'

'Um. More forethought than I would have given him credit for,' admitted Carol reluctantly.

But Erica wasn't listening.

'I must run out to the call-box at the corner, and ring him up now. I *must* thank him to-night.'

'Don't have more than ten-pennorth of conversation,' Carol called after her. 'You ought to be in bed early. It's your last day at the office to-morrow, remember, and good-byes are always exhausting.'

Erica promised absently as she slipped on her coat, and ran down the steps of the old-fashioned house.

But as she did so someone came in quickly at the gate, and she rushed straight into him.

'Oliver! I'm sorry.'

'Why?' His arms went round her instinctively for a moment. 'It's quite appropriate that you should fling yourself into my arms at this juncture.'

Erica laughed. And then suddenly she put up her hands round his face.

'Oliver, I did want to fling myself into your arms, really. You see, I've just——'

'Don't!' He sharply jerked back from her hands, and her voice trailed off into dismayed silence.

'I don't understand,' she whispered at last, appalled to see all the old, dark melancholy in his face again.

'I'm sorry.' He spoke in a hard, expressionless voice. 'I shouldn't have done it like that. But I don't want your—sweet ways. I can do without them. They're not in the bargain.'

Erica fell away from him.

'I wasn't thinking of any bargain,' she said, with a proud little quiver in her tone. 'I was only—I was only——' She turned away suddenly, unable to finish the sentence.

'What, Erica?' He was behind her now, one hand on her shoulder, but she only shook her head. 'Tell me—— Why, you're crying! I didn't mean to make you cry. What was it you wanted to do?'

'Only to thank you for your present,' she whispered. 'It's just come, and I thought—I thought I'd like to thank you for it right away.'

34

'Oh, my child——' She was suddenly drawn right into his arms. 'Forgive me. I can't explain. . . . It was when you did that—put your hands against my face. It brought back——'

He stopped short, but he had no need to continue. Erica thought in a flash of furious, hurt comprehension: '*She* used to do that. I'll never do it again.'

And then, like a cold hand on her heart, came the thought, 'Even a gesture which reminds him of her has the power to stir him to the depths.'

She was quite calm now. She accepted his apology very gently. There was nothing for him to worry about. It was all forgotten.

Would he come in?

No, he had only brought a message which had been left at his home by mistake instead of at hers.

And that was all?

Yes, that was all.

Then they would say good night. There was nothing else to bother about.

They said good night, with a touch of restraint in spite of the protestations, and Erica went back into the house, rather more slowly than she had come out.

'Well,' Carol wanted to know, 'was he pleased to have your thanks?'

'Yes, he was pleased,' Erica said. But she didn't enlarge on the subject, and very soon she went to bed.

The next day was tiring, as Carol had said it would be, for the good-byes were something of a strain. Besides, Erica felt depressed. She badly wanted reassuring, and there was no one to reassure her. Only people who laughed and teased good-naturedly, and openly envied her the wealth that was going to be hers.

They had no suspicion that anything could be wrong—she had no intention that they should, of course. To them she was simply the fortunate girl who had attracted the notice of her wealthy employer.

Very romantic really, wasn't it? And wasn't she a lucky girl? Everyone said practically the same thing over and over again as she went round to each department in turn.

Erica supposed it was always a little melancholy doing this sort of thing, but she wished it hadn't been quite such an effort to agree brightly that yes, she *was* a lucky girl, and it was lovely to be leaving the office.

'It isn't a bit lovely,' she thought with a sigh, as she got back to her own room again. 'I've been very happy here nearly all the time. I *hate* to think of someone else doing all the things for Oliver that I've always done.'

She felt silly and jealous about her own dear little office where she had planned so many things and done so much work for him. Perhaps there wouldn't be so much opportunity for her to look after him now. After all, it was at the office that he spent most of his day and——

'Finshed all the good-byes?'

She turned, smiling a little then, to find Oliver standing in the doorway.

'Yes. Every one of them.'

'Except to your employer himself.'

'Oh'—she laughed a little. 'We'd beter take that as said, hadn't we?'

'Not at all. I don't part with a secretary of your attributes in that casual manner.' He was smiling, but she had the odd impression that he was nervous.

'Why, what are you going to do? Make a farewell speech?'

'I ought to—enumerating your virtues, oughtn't I?'

'No. You did that once before,' she told him.

'Did I?' He looked surprised. 'When?'

'When I first became your secretary. You said I was quick and conscientious and intelligent and—and faithful.'

'Really? I didn't know I knew so much about you then. But it was all true. And I hate losing you, Miss Murril.'

'I hate going, Mr. Leyne,' she said earnestly.

'I wanted to make you a—a parting gift to show you my appreciation.' The nervousness deepened suddenly, and he took a small jewel case from his pocket.

She watched in silence while he struggled to open it with his gloved hand. She knew then he must be nervous or he would have remembered to use the other hand, but she didn't make the mistake of offering to help him. And presently the case was open.

'Oh, Oliver, you shouldn't!' She looked at the little diamond and platinum watch with something between laughter and tears. He put it into her hands, and she held it very lightly and tenderly.

'Thank you. It's heavenly.' She didn't know what else to say, when she remembered the scene last night.

And then she saw he was staring boyishly at the ground.

'It—it's because I spoilt the other present, you know,' he said.

'Oh, how absurd of you!' She laughed tremulously and just patted his arm, because she dared not do more. But she thought in her heart that nothing else would ever be half so precious as this little diamond watch he had given her.

Quite often, during the last few weeks, she had gone with Oliver to the big house in the evenings, and she had discovered that he was more than willing that she should spend as much money as she liked on altering the place.

'I think it's hateful as it is,' he told her, 'but I don't know quite what it needs.'

Erica knew, however, and she was amused and touched at the way he received her suggestions. Even in a few weeks she managed to make a good deal of difference, and Oliver's own study was a beautiful place by the time she had finished with it.

They were there on the evening after her good-bye to the office, and he had been looking round with an air of complete satisfaction.

'I like this room now,' he remarked thoughtfully. 'There's something very different about it. How did you do it?'

He came and leant his arms on the back of the chair, and smiled down at her. But before she could reply a servant came in with the evening mail, and told Oliver that someone was waiting to see him.

'Would you like to look through whatever is there, Erica? I don't expect I shall be long,' he said as he went out of the room.

Erica pushed aside one or two files which they had brought from the office because they had been working out

37

some details of a business deal together, and drew the pile of letters towards her.

She felt very happy, sitting there in Oliver's study, already most strangely at home. They had had a fire lit because the late September evening was chilly, and the firelight cast a cosy and intimate glow on the deep gold and brown shades of the furniture.

Two or three of the letters, although from people she did not know, contained cordial wishes for their future happiness. And that, too, gave her a warm little feeling at her heart.

The last letter of the pile was addressed in an obviously feminine handwriting and posted from Paris.

Erica hesitated a moment, but Oliver had told her to open everything, and she thought she remembered his saying he had distant relatives abroad.

The thin grey note-paper was headed from a famous hotel, and the letter started without preamble:

'Oliver dear, Don't think me too much of a ghost from the past, but so often in the last year I have wanted to write to you. Now I have gathered my courage to do so.'

Apparently an old friend who had heard of his approaching marriage and now had broken a long silence with a note of congratulation.

Erica read on idly, expecting the usual stereotyped phrases. But suddenly her attention became riveted.

'... I've finished my summer concert tour now. It's been roses all the way, quite literally—the sort of thing we dreamed of in the old days.... Shall be in England for a while now.... In London most of the time.... Couldn't we meet just once? You see, I'm being quite humble about it.... Unless the past is too much past to you for it to matter any more.'

And then, right at the end:

'How shall I sign myself? I feel I hardly know. And

38

yet—yes, I do. For the sake of the past, and perhaps a little for the future, too—With all my love, DREDA.'

Erica sprang to her feet, instinctively crumpling up the letter in her hand. She felt panic-stricken, and furious too. How dared this woman stretch out a hand from the past and try to snatch Oliver back to the misery she had caused him before?

He had been almost tranquil lately—almost happy, except for that one time when he had been reminded of Dreda. Was that all to be carelessly crushed and thrown aside because some woman's vanity must be ministered to?

'I couldn't build it again,' Erica thought desperately. 'It's so very, very fragile. I haven't had time to strengthen it. This woman could kill it with a glance and a couple of words.'

And then, with a fierce protectiveness that swamped all other feeling—'She shall *not*!'

There was no need for him ever to see the letter. '... unless the past is too much past to you for it to matter any more.' If Dreda received no answer she would draw the obvious conclusion—that he was so angry and uncaring that he would not even answer.

It was simple. It was perfectly simple. Erica put out her hand to the fire.

And then with a gasp of dismay she drew it back.

What did she think she was doing? Committing the meanest and lowest of all deceptions, tampering with someone else's letters. And he trusted her, absolutely. It never entered his head that his letters were not just as safe with her as with him.

She had let this passion for protection fog her sense of values. That letter had been written by Dreda for Oliver. It was for Oliver to decide what should be done with it.

Erica felt the slow tears gathering behind her aching eyelids. Sobbing under her breath, she tried, not very successfully, to smooth out the crumpled sheet.

And if Oliver's decision set her outside his life once more?

Well, that, too, was something which he himself must decide. She couldn't help any of them by cheating over the facts.

The telephone bell rang sharply, making her start guiltily. She put down Dreda's letter on the desk and went over to take the receiver.

'Hello.'

She could not infuse much interest into her voice, and when she found it was the builder who was carrying out the alterations to the house she had an hysterical desire to say:

'It doesn't really matter. They may not be needed after all.'

Oliver was coming back now. She could hear his footsteps along the passage. In less than a minute he would have Dreda's letter. This dear firelit room would be cosy and peaceful no longer. It would be full of drama and tenseness.

She tried to keep her mind on what was being said to her, but it was almost beyond her power.

And then he was in the room, humming a little in a contented way, an unlighted cigarette between his lips. He smiled across at her and felt in his pockets for his lighter.

It was maddening, watching him waste time over a trifle like that when almost their lives hung in the balance. And, in the end, he seemed unable to find the lighter.

She saw him give an idle glance at the desk. Then suddenly she became completely deaf to what was being said on the telephone.

He absently picked up the crumpled sheet of paper and was making it into a spill.

Erica watched in a sort of horrified fascination, while it seemed to her that fate itself took the decision out of her hands.

She never knew afterwards whether she tried to find her voice and it just physically failed her, or whether she acted deliberately. It was like the kind of dream where you couldn't even cry out.

Oliver bent down to the fire, and a little flame curled up round the twist of paper. He straightened up and lighted his

40

cigarette, the spill burning almost to his fingers as he did so. Then he tossed the charred end back into the fire.

In silence, Erica replaced the receiver.

'Anything of interest in the post?' asked Oliver as she came over to the fire.

'No,' Erica told him steadily. 'Nothing of interest in the post.'

CHAPTER II

VERY much later that night, when she was in bed, Erica
allowed her thoughts to go slowly back over the events of
the evening.

She didn't possess the kind of conscience that could be
quieted with a word, and, for some terrible moments, she
wondered if she had ruined her happiness instead of saving
it by what she had done.

It was useless to argue that matters had been taken out of
her hands, she told herself ruthlessly. That was only shirking the question on a technical detail.

The only real question was—Did the ultimate right
justify the present wrong?

Carol, breathing away contentedly in her bed the other
side of the room, would almost certainly have burnt the
letter herself without a qualm—and then have slept as
tranquilly as she was doing now. But then Carol had never
looked at these things in the same way as Erica.

It was rather tempting to waken her now and put the
whole thing before her. Erica knew what her verdict would
be, only she terribly wanted to be convinced herself.

But why wake Carol for nothing? She thought the next
minute. It would be impossible to explain the exact situation between Oliver and Dreda. Come to that, she was not
so very clear about it herself.

Carol would merely think it was a case of an old flame
turning up at an awkward moment. Remedy—put out the
flame.

It didn't entirely answer the problem, but it finally sent
Erica to sleep with the incident of the letter banished uneasily to the back of her mind. And there it remained for
the whole of the strange week that followed.

On the night before her wedding, Carol insisted in sending her to bed early.

'How do I know what rest you'll get after this—rushing

about Paris and Milan and Verona, or wherever it is?'

'I think it's supposed to be a lazy honeymoon,' Erica protested mildly. But she was glad to do what Carol told her, all the same.

She thought she must surely lie awake, worrying over the strange step she was taking. But she did nothing of the sort. She slept dreamlessly and tranquilly—to wake to brilliant sunshine and the realisation that to-day she was to marry Oliver.

Carol was in her element. She adored weddings—'even a poky, early-morning one like this in an empty church.' And she stood by in admiring delight while Erica put on the pastel-green suit with the deep sable cuffs—which was the most extravagant thing she had ever worn in her life.

'Honestly, Erica, you look good enough to eat. That little green hat on your chestnut hair is the sweetest thing. I only hope he appreciates you.'

Erica didn't say anything. She only smiled because, though she didn't want to talk herself, she rather liked the sound of Carol's running commentary as a background to her own tumultuous thoughts.

Then, just as she was ready, a knock on the door heralded the arrival of Oliver's chauffeur, who was to drive the two girls to the church.

Erica picked up the sheaf of pinky cream roses which Oliver had sent her, and went out to the car, rather touched by the smile of admiration which the chauffeur gave her.

'The staff all send you their good wishes, madam,' he said, as he put a rug over her knees.

'Thank you, Marriott.' Erica returned his smile a little shyly. And then they were off on the incredible ten minutes' journey which was to end in her marriage to Oliver.

'I, Erica, take thee, Oliver, to my wedded husband ... for better for worse ... for richer for poorer ... in sickness and in health ... till death us do part. ...'

Erica used to wonder afterwards whether it was really her own voice that spoke so clearly and firmly. It seemed to come almost without her own volition, and to hold in it a promise of confidence and sincerity.

'They're such lovely words,' thought Erica. 'They say just what I want to say. I wish I could repeat them all over again to him when we are alone.'

But, of course, there would be no question of that.

'With this ring I thee wed...'

She gazed at the thin gold circlet that was being placed on her finger. Strange how much that little ring meant. Their whole lives were now contained in it.

She could feel Oliver's hand, very steady on hers, and she thought, 'I'm glad he's perfectly calm about these things. I should hate to have a husband who is easily put out, even if Oliver does go to the other extreme sometimes.'

And then it was all over, and Carol was kissing her, and giving herself the exquisite and impertinent pleasure of addressing her chief as 'Oliver.'

Oliver seemed to be taking it extremely well, and presently he put his arm round Erica and drew her aside to introduce her to his best man. Colin Lamb was a tall, pleasant man, with a cynical mouth and kindly eyes.

'He hasn't any illusions himself, but he's rather nice about other people's,' thought Erica. 'I can imagine he would be a good friend.'

Apparently he had known Oliver for many years, and when Erica heard that he had actually come all the way from Vienna for the express purpose of attending their wedding, she was genuinely touched and pleased.

'Do you live in Vienna, then?' she asked, as they moved in a group out into the porch.

'Oh, no, but a good many of my engagements are in Austria. Chamber music, you know. That was how I first met Oliver,' he explained, not specially lucidly, Erica thought.

'Oh, I see.' She wondered a little what Oliver had to do with chamber music, but just then the car drove up once more and there was no opportunity of any further enquiries.

They drove to one of the big hotels, where a champagne breakfast had been ordered. Of the four, Carol probably enjoyed herself the most. Such things did not usually come her way, and, as she remarked, '*I* haven't been making any silly promises I might regret.'

'Miss Shawn is, I take it, something of a pessimist where marriage is concerned?' said Colin Lamb with a little bow to her.

'Well——' began Carol.

'Please don't prejudice Erica at the outset,' begged Oliver amusedly. 'She is probably turning over all her own misgivings at the moment.'

'Misgivings? Erica hasn't got any misgivings. She thinks this marriage is the most wonderful thing that ever happened,' said Carol, in a tone which showed her own opinion of it rather distressingly well.

'Really? I am happy to hear that my wife feels so confident of the future.' And Oliver smiled at Erica over the rim of his glass.

But Erica blushed and wished nervously that Carol would keep off such dangerous ground. It was difficult to know what she would say next, because she was obviously divided between pleasurable awe at being there at all, and a desire to make the party entirely her own by some outrageous and amusing remark.

However, the meal passed off without any other difficult moments, and, almost at once, it seemed it was time for them to go.

Marriott was to drive them both to the big house to collect the luggage, and then on to the station to catch the London train. From there they were to go by the evening plane to Paris, on the first stage of their honeymoon.

It was all utterly strange and impossible, Erica thought, but deliciously strange and impossible, too.

Saying good-bye to Carol made her very serious for a moment, but she had to smile again at the warm kiss and the whispered, 'Bless you. Be very happy. He doesn't seem so bad, after all.'

No so bad, after all.

She glanced at him when they were alone in the car together. He was leaning back, looking out of the window with that faint, almost happy smile. And she thought:

'He's the dearest thing in the world. And he's my husband.'

As they came up the drive, the sun was shining brilliantly, and for once the house looked mellow instead of gloomy.

'How nice the place is looking,' Erica exclaimed.

He raised his eyebrows slightly in surprise, and then said, 'Why, yes, I suppose it is. I never remember thinking that of it before.'

'That's because it's really home now,' thought Erica, but she decided it was best not to say anything like that.

The car drew to a standstill.

'Will you come in? Or is it not worth while for a minute?'

'I'll stay out here, Oliver.'

'All right. I shall only be a little while.'

Both Oliver and the chauffeur went into the house, and Erica leant back in the car, studying the sunlight in the yellowing leaves. She knew suddenly why the old man had had such a pride and pleasure in the place. It was so different when you *belonged*.

She saw his point about wanting someone to whom it could all be passed on. Until now she had always thought that he was a little absurd, but——

Erica turned her head sharply as, with a self-advertising 'zoom,' a cream and scarlet sports car shot up the drive. It did everything but peel the paint off the side of the waiting car, and came to an abrupt stop immediately in front of the flight of steps.

At the exact moment that Oliver appeared once more at the top of the steps, out of the car climbed an incredibly pretty and smart young woman.

She wore tailored white linen and her head was bare. But far more marvellous than any hat was her wonderful red hair. It was flaming and audacious—and utterly beautiful.

She stood there, smiling up challengingly at Oliver in the sunlight, and it needed no pallor of his to tell Erica with fatal certainty. This was Dreda.

He came slowly down the steps, pausing half a second on each one. But by the time he reached the bottom his composure was complete again.

'Why, Dreda, this is a surprise. You were the last person I expected to see here.'

'And is it a pleasant surprise?'

'Of course.' His voice was a little formal. 'But come and meet my wife.'

'Your—*wife*?'

Erica felt bound to admire the magnificent way she took the shock. For a moment her wonderful lashes flickered almost nervously, and then she said, 'I had no idea you were married, Oliver. How exciting.'

'Yes, isn't it? You are just in time to congratulate us. We were married this morning.'

That, too, must have been a terrible shock—to know that she had lost by so narrow a margin—but she looked quite composed as Oliver brought her over to the car.

He was wonderfully cool, too, as he introduced 'Miss Canterley' to Erica, and she saw that his hand was perfectly steady as it rested on the window-ledge of the car.

'She's everything I thought—and feared,' reflected Erica nervously, while Dreda's almost black eyes flicked over her contemptuously, and then dismissed her as negligible.

'So you're starting on your honeymoon to-day?' Dreda was smiling again at Oliver in that almost terrifying way. '*Now* I see why you didn't even bother to answer my letter.'

It was bound to come, of course, since she had had the effrontery even to come to the house unasked, but at that remark, Erica thought they must surely hear her very heart-beats.

'Letter? What letter?' Oliver gave a puzzled little frown.

'The one I sent from Paris, of course.' For a moment Dreda was not perfectly mistress of herself, and her voice sharpened a trifle.

'It's the end,' thought Erica. 'In a few seconds he will know.' And she wished she could just die quietly and quickly.

But Oliver remained unaware of the crisis.

'I had no letter from you, my dear.' And then, with a very faint smile, 'I'm afraid it's the old story, Dreda. It's not the first time you've addressed a letter with your mind on something else quite different. I seem to remember other letters going astray.'

'No, no. I *know* it was properly addressed. I took such

47

care with it because——'

'You begin to make me very curious, and very sorry that I've missed your letter,' Oliver said lightly. But, in spite of the tone of his voice, Erica noticed that by now he was gripping the frame of the window nervously. He was wondering, of course, what *had* been in the letter. And *she* was wondering into whose hands it had fallen.

And the girl who could have answered both questions sat very still and prayed that the storm would not break. It seemed impossible to her that they would accept the rather feeble explanation. Indeed, Dreda was extremely reluctant to do anything of the sort.

'It's simply absurd. The letter must be somewhere,' she began. And then, suddenly, she seemed to realise that she was losing her dignity badly at a time when she needed it. She made a tremendous effort, and somehow recovered her calm.

'Well, never mind,' she said casually. 'It doesn't really matter. And perhaps'—her wicked eyes travelled over Erica and then returned to Oliver—'perhaps in view of what's happened to-day, it's just as well that it did go astray.'

And she laughed.

It was that, Erica saw, which riveted Oliver's attention as nothing else had. She almost expected him to take hold of Dreda and demand to know what that letter had contained.

But before he could satisfy himself by the most casual enquiry, Dreda cleverly snatched away the chance before his eyes. She said very coolly:

'But I must let you go now. It's unpardonable to delay a man on his honeymoon. And in any case I shall still be in this part of the world when you return. Where are you going—or is it a secret?'

'No, it's no secret.' Oliver spoke with a slight but obvious effort. 'We're going to Italy—Verona most of the time.'

'Verona?' Dreda repeated the word indescribably, making it sound like music. 'It's the place of all places I would choose for a honeymoon—the most romantic spot on earth.'

'Yes.' Oliver spoke almost harshly. 'Erica wanted very much to see it. And I—I wanted to show it to her.'

'Of course.' The faintest touch of wistfulness made Dreda's smile doubly beautiful. 'How I envy you—Erica.'

Somehow Erica found a conventional reply to that, though she scarcely knew what she said herself. And then Dreda looked at her curiously and said:

'Do you know, I can't remember a single Erica among our set in the old days. But perhaps you came to the district after I left England?'

'Yes, I think I did. But in any case, I didn't meet Oliver socially, you know. I was his secretary.'

'His *secretary*? Were you? Then you're one of these really clever people. You actually dealt with his business affairs and—his letters?'

'To a certain extent—yes.'

'How interesting,' Dreda said slowly, her smiling eyes never leaving Erica's face. 'So you dealt with his letters. I *see*.'

And with a sudden fear that made her heart feel like lead, Erica wondered just how much Dreda *had* seen.

She scarcely heard the perfunctory good-byes which were exchanged, or knew that she and Oliver had started on their honeymoon at last. She only seemed to hear the cold suspicion in Dreda's voice and see the look of frightening speculation in her eyes.

It was a little better when she and Oliver were alone in the train together. Every minute then was taking them further away from Dreda, and perhaps they need never see her again. After all, she had been away from the district for years. She might——

Then Erica remembered that fatal, careless remark—'I shall still be in this part of the world when you return.'

That wasn't what she had intended, according to her letter. Something had changed her mind now. Something not unconnected with Oliver.

Erica listened to the thrumming of the train wheels and thought it sounded menacing. Later, she listened to the noise of the plane and thought that sounded menacing too. But all the time she knew there was something much more frightening than either of those vague fancies. And that was Oliver's silence.

49

He was not a talkative man. She hadn't expected him to be voluble. But this wordless preoccupation, from which he tried conscientiously to rouse himself from time to time, could only have one meaning. He was wondering—he *must* be wondering—what that letter had said. And after that, he must be asking himself if Dreda had made some overture which he would gladly have accepted had he known.

'I wonder if any girl ever had such a strange beginning to her honeymoon,' thought Erica unhappily.

In Paris they drove to one of the big hotels for the night. But the name made Erica shudder, for it was the name that had headed the letter from Dreda.

A beautiful suite was engaged for her, and Erica tried to tell herself that it was lovely to live in luxury like this. But it was not really lovely at all. She cried herself to sleep in a bed fit for an empress, and presumably Oliver lay awake in something equally magnificent and tormented himself with thoughts of Dreda.

It was no more than Oliver's proposal had strictly implied, but somehow the full realisation of what strangers they were to remain chilled and dismayed Erica beyond expression.

The next day they went on—though in her heart Erica was beginning to feel that she wanted to rush back to England instead and somehow undo all this crazy mistake which they had made.

Another night in another magnificent hotel—this time in Milan—did less than nothing to reassure her, and Oliver seemed such a stranger by now that she thought she would not have been surprised if he had addressed her as 'Miss Murril.' Never in her life had she known such depression as she felt in the hired car, speeding over the historic Plain of Lombardy towards Verona.

'Erica.'

She looked across at him.

'How pale and quiet you are.'

'Am I? It's—it's the heat,' she stammered.

'Yes, I know.' There was a curious little undercurrent in his voice that made it sound very gentle. 'It's been a long journey. But we shall soon be there now. It will be quite different then.'

'Will it?' she said a little sadly.

'I *promise* you.' And suddenly she realised from the urgency in his tone what he was trying to tell her.

He was sorry. He knew he had been moody, and now he was trying to reassure her, though he could not quite put it into words.

'Oh, I do understand, dear. I do understand,' she wanted to tell him. But she knew she must not put it into words either.

So, instead, with her heart feeling lighter than it had since she had seen Dreda, she smiled across brilliantly at him and said:

'I know I'm going to love the place, and we'll have a wonderful time.'

And although he said no more, he gave her a queerly grateful little look that scarcely left her memory once during the next few days.

It was perfectly true—she did love Verona from the first moment. She didn't know which was the most beautiful time of the day: the bright sunny mornings, when they wandered in the tangled grounds of the Castelvecchio, and watched the tiny lizards running up and down the warm stone walls. The still, languorous siesta of mid-day, when every sound in the place seemed to cease, and even the children were silent. The lengthening shadows of late afternoon, when out came the brown-skinned *bambini* once more to play in the gardens of the Piazza Bra. Or the warm, purple twilight that gradually deepened over the ancient city until it seemed that a velvet curtain was hanging overhead.

And it was not only her own pleasure but Oliver's too that seemed to increase as each day passed. The Italian sunlight appeared sufficient to charm away even the shadow of Dreda, and Erica dared to hope again.

Two weeks of their honeymoon had slipped away, and Erica was beginning to tell herself that this pleasant, unemotional comradeship between them was to last for ever. If sometimes her heart cried out for something else—something with a little more of ecstacy and a little more of

51

danger about it—she tried to believe that this solid, reliable friendship would probably be a stronger weapon against Dreda in the end. At least there was nothing in it that he could distrust.

And then one night, when she was almost ready for bed, he came and knocked on the door that divided their two rooms.

She turned sharply from the dressing-table where she was sitting.

'Yes—come in.'

He opened the door and came into the room, looking so perfectly calm that her own self-possession returned at once. Oliver in a dressing-gown could look just as cool and businesslike as Oliver in a morning suit. It made her want to smile just to see it.

'May I borrow your fountain pen, Erica? I seem to have mislaid mine.'

'Of course.' She turned back to the glass and began to brush her hair. 'You'll find it beside my writing-case over there.'

'Thank you.'

'But must you really write letters at this time of night?' She leant her bare arm on the back of the chair again, her hairbrush still in her hand. 'It's very late, Oliver.'

'I know.' He picked up the pen. 'But it's almost too hot to sleep, even without that to keep one awake.' He amusedly jerked his head towards the open window, from beyond which came sounds of clinking glasses and gay Latin voices singing.

Erica smiled too.

'I know. It's almost too much of a good thing when you're tired. But in the ordinary way, I love to lie in bed and listen to them singing. They're quite indefatigable.'

Oliver stood leaning against the side of the window, looking out into the warm darkness.

'Yes, give an Italian a chance to sit out under the stars and sing about love, and he's perfectly happy. He can keep it up for hours. I imagine that's why Italy's supposed to be the most wonderful honeymoon country on earth.'

'Well, I think it is.'

He laughed then, and came over to where she was sitting.

'Satisfied with your honeymoon?'

'Of course. More than satisfied.' But she didn't look at him now—not even at his reflection in the glass.

'What lovely hair you have, Erica,' he said slowly, and put out his hand to touch it.

She was so astonished at the change in his voice that she turned suddenly to look up at him, and as she did so his gloved hand came against her neck.

It was his turn to look startled. Startled and almost resentful.

'I'm sorry,' he said quickly, and she was struck by something a little apprehensive in his voice.

'It's all right, Oliver,' she said, not quite understanding. 'You can touch my hair if you like. Why not?'

'It wasn't that.' He spoke very low, almost sullenly.

'What, then?'

'I put—my hand—against your neck. I'm sorry, it was an accident. I never meant to touch you with it at all. I know how—horrible it is.'

'Don't!' Erica felt she could not bear those jerky, hurt little sentences. 'It's not horrible at all. I don't mind your poor hand, my dear. What sort of a beast do you think I am?'

'It's very natural to hate it,' he muttered.

'Oh, no. See—I don't mind it at all.' She took his hand very gently and put it against her neck, holding it there and smiling at him a little.

His eyes became dark and enormous, and she saw that his lips had gone rather dry.

'Don't you—really mind? Is that the truth?'

'Of course.'

He dropped on his knees beside her suddenly and buried his head against her.

'But you must. *Any* woman would hate it.'

'Oh, no.' She wanted to add, 'Only Dreda,' but she managed not to.

'Two of the fingers are missing, you know. Do you still not mind?' She felt that he was trembling slightly.

'No, of course not.'

'I don't understand,' he whispered, pressing his head against her so that he almost hurt her.

She stroked his hair very gently and held him close.

'But I've always known that your hand was hurt, and though I've always been sorry for your sake, it couldn't possibly affect my—liking for you. Why should it? Only someone very shallow and absurd would mind.'

'Oh, no,' he said sadly. 'You're an angel to feel like that, but most people don't.'

She saw it was useless to argue with his obsession just then, and so she said, instead:

'I think your hands must have meant a very great deal to you once, and that's why it all seems out of proportion to you.'

'Yes, of course,' he said a little impatiently, as though she ought to know all about that anyway.

'Won't you tell me how it happened?'

'Yes, if you like. I thought perhaps you knew.' He turned his head, but he didn't move from her arms, so that he lay still with his cheek against her. She could see how pale he was, and how wide and dark his eyes were, but that look of tragedy had lessened.

'It was at the Works, seven or eight years ago. That's really why I hate them so much.'

'Yes?' Erica's voice was even more soothing than the touch of her hand.

'I never wanted to go into the business at all. I couldn't understand my father's overwhelming passion for it. All I wanted to be was a concert pianist. It wasn't just a silly boyish fancy. My whole heart and soul was in it, and my masters declared I had a brilliant future if I went on with it.'

'But you had the misfortune to be the only son,' Erica suggested softly.

'Exactly.'

A good many things were falling into their place for Erica now. She saw the common ground on which Dreda and Oliver had met—and she saw why it was that he and his father had never liked each other.

He sighed impatiently and stirred a little against her.

54

'If ever I had a son, he should choose his own path for himself. It's terrible to try to live your children's lives for them.'

'Yes, I agree with you.' Erica still spoke very calmly, but she wondered a little if he realised what 'if ever I had a son' implied.

'There were endless rows,' Oliver went on slowly. 'But in the end we came to a compromise. I agreed to go into the business for two years and learn the whole thing from the beginning. My father was certain that, once what he called "my ridiculous notions" were put in the right perspective, he would have no more trouble. It was terrible to have to confine my own absorbing interest to my very limited spare time. But I managed it, and devoted all my energies to the business.'

'And did it make any difference in your feelings?' Erica lightly passed her hand over his hair again.

'No, not at all. I stuck out the two years. I think I was absolutely honest and conscientious about it—I tried to be—but in my heart I always looked forward to escaping at the end of that time. I had to satisfy my father—perhaps he had a right to expect that—but he had promised that if, at the end, I still felt the same, I should follow my own wishes.

'And then——' He hesitated a moment, then went on without much expression: 'About a couple of months before the end of the two years, I was going through the Works one day with my father. We stopped to watch a new piece of machinery in the working. I don't know now what happened. I don't think the man was careless—it was just that failure of the human element which happens once or twice in a million. Anyway, it doesn't matter now. Something had gone wrong, I could see, and I only had a half second to act. The man would have been killed if I hadn't —so it had to be my hand instead.'

Erica was very still.

'You mean—you deliberately sacrificed your hand to save his life?' she said at last.

'It wasn't exactly that, Erica.' He smiled faintly. 'I'm afraid there was nothing heroic about it like that. It was just as instinctive movement that anyone would have made to stop a man being killed. I don't expect I even visualised the consequences.'

'Nothing heroic about it?' Erica repeated slowly, and, gently taking his injured hand, she put her lips against it.

'Erica——' He stared at her incredulously. Then he suddenly snatched his hand away and cast his arms round her. 'How *can* you? You're so absurd and sweet.'

She laughed a little at that, and then he kissed her.

'May I—stay here with you? There's such comfort where you are,' he said simply.

'Why, my dear——' She didn't even finish the sentence. She didn't have to. The light in her eyes did that for her. And without a word, he picked her right up in his arms.

It was absurd—it was absurd that she should think of Dreda then. But by the very height of her happiness at that moment, she seemed to measure the terrifying depths to which she could be cast.

Hours afterwards, when he was sleeping against her with the tranquillity of a child, she lay watching the stars slowly fade before the dawn. And she asked herself how much one night could weigh in the balance against his years of romantic devotion to Dreda.

CHAPTER III

'CAROL! Carol, where are you?'

Erica stood in the tiny hall of the flat, smiling, a little breathless and tremendously excited.

Carol came running out of the kitchenette.

'Darling girl, how lovely to see you! When did you get back?'

'This afternoon. And I suddenly found that I still had my key of the flat, so I thought I'd come along and surprise you.'

Carol kissed her very heartily and then held her at arm's length.

'Ye-es.' She looked critically at her. 'I should say the honeymoon agreed with you all right. You look a bit grave, but I dare say that's the new status of married woman weighing on you rather heavily.'

Erica smiled. 'Don't be absurd. I'm not at all grave.'

Carol nodded. 'Oh, yes. But then you always were, so never mind about that now. Come and sit down and tell me all about it. Or rather, of course, you won't do anything of the sort. Like all honeymooners, you'll sigh romantically over the high spots, and draw a discreet veil over anything like the first quarrel. I don't blame you. It must always be humiliating to have to admit that one honeymoon is just like any other one.'

'Sorry to disappoint you. There hasn't *been* a first quarrel,' Erica assured her with a laugh.

'Not? That's a bad sign,' Carol said darkly. 'The longer you leave it, the bigger the explosion. You'd better work up something the moment you get back home.'

Erica leant back in her chair and looked contentedly round.

'It's nice to hear your nonsense again. I missed you, Carol.'

'I'm sure you did.' Carol looked gratified. 'I suppose

you've had to rely on iron and steel for your chief topic of conversation, with an occasional visit to a picture gallery and a discussion on the Italian primitives as a really dashing interlude.'

'Oh, no.' Erica shook her head with a smile. 'We did quite a lot of things that even you would have approved of, I'm sure.'

'And Oliver is a marvellous husband?'

'Oliver is a marvellous husband,' Erica agreed, with her smile becoming very tender.

'Well, of course, I don't know that that's much to go by,' Carol said sceptically. '*You* always said he was a marvellous employer, but I never remember anyone else rushing to support the verdict.'

'All of which means you're trying to disguise the fact that you're sentimentally thrilled at finding my marriage a success,' Erica accused her with a laugh.

'All right.' Carol grinned. 'I really am awfully glad, dear.'

'I know.' Erica looked at her affectionately. 'And how are things at the office?'

'Is this the wife of my boss speaking?' Carol wanted to know. 'Or the ex-private secretary?'

'Neither. Just your own friend.'

'Oh, well—the office is all right as far as I'm concerned. That's to say, I don't hate it any more than usual.'

'And apart from you?'

'So-so. I don't think your successor is going to be a howling success.'

'Don't you?' Erica looked anxious. 'But it's unfair to judge her yet, and anyway you can't have seen much of her.'

'No. But I have a peculiar aptitude for recognising the natural nitwit at sight. I recognised her.'

Erica laughed, but she still looked worried.

'Anyway, what does a little muddle more or less at the office matter to you now?' Carol wanted to know. 'You won't have to clear up the mess. Your part nowadays is merely to stroll into the office late in the afternoon and engage Oliver in conversation, just when all the staff are hoping to goodness he'll sign the letters quickly. If the wives of bosses only knew how they court poison in their office cup of tea when they hold up the post!'

'Yes, I know,' murmured Erica feelingly. 'At least, I'll never do that. But I do hope this girl turns out all right. It will worry Oliver so much if not.'

'Well, let him do his own worrying, darling. And, any-way, if she's a flop you can always come back and be his temporary aid and guide until he finds another treasure like you.'

'That's true.' Erica smiled thoughtfully. 'Of course, you know, that's just exactly what I should like to do.'

'Yes, I know. You're that sort of idiot, if you'll excuse my saying so,' Carol said.

'Don't you think it's natural to want to work for a man when you love him?'

'No, I don't. I think it's much more natural to want to make him work for you. If he's got your love he ought to be so pleased with his luck that he's willing to work all the harder,' declared Carol ruthlessly.

'You're hopeless.' Erica got up with a little laugh. 'I must go. I promised Oliver I would be back to dinner.'

'Erica——' Carol hesitated. 'There's just one thing I want to say to you.'

'Yes?' Erica looked a little surprised at the change of tone.

'It's not my business, and it's not specially important, I expect, but if I don't tell you some kind friend will. The girl Oliver was engaged to before is back here.'

There was a moment's silence. Then Erica said with an effort, 'Yes, I know.'

'You know! Oh, then I needn't have bothered.'

Erica didn't answer that directly. She said instead:

'How did you know, Carol? I mean, how was it that the subject was brought up at all?'

'She came to the office.'

'To the *office*?' Erica's calm forsook her for the moment. 'But why? What could she want?'

'I know, that's just what I thought. It was why I felt perhaps it was best to tell you,' Carol said seriously. 'You see, I saw her. And she's—well, stunning is the only word.'

'I know that, too,' Erica answered without much expression.

'Do you mean *you* have seen her?'

'Yes.'

'When?'

Again Erica hesitated. And then she said:

'On our wedding day. She—came to the house and I saw her for a moment.'

'Good heavens.' Carol looked exceedingly dismayed. 'What did she want there?'

Erica frowned.

'She—didn't know Oliver was married. I suppose she just happened to come and look him up then.'

'Happened!' Carol was scornful. 'I dare say she just *happened* to see about old Leyne's will when it was published.'

'Oh——'

'What?'

'Nothing.' Erica had gone a little white. Was it rather more than coincidence that the letter from Dreda should have followed so promptly on the old man's death? she wondered. Then she pulled herself together. It was no good fancying things and getting panicky.

'Anyway, now she realises that Oliver is married, she'll probably take a different view of things,' Erica said.

'It was *after* that that she came to the office,' Carol reminded her reluctantly. 'She came in as though the place belonged to her, on the date you were originally expected back. It was only because you stayed away a day or two longer that she missed him.'

'And you saw her, you say?'

'Yes. I happened to be seeing the new secretary about a query, and in she came. I must say she took the disappointment well.'

'Yes,' Erica said a trifle drily. 'She's magnificent in defeat. That's why I'm afraid of her.'

'*Are* you afraid, Erica?'

'Just a little.'

'I don't think you need worry, really, dear,' Carol

assured her earnestly. 'I wouldn't have said anything, only it's always best to know when that man-eating type is about.'

Erica smiled faintly.

'Yes, I would rather know,' she agreed with a sigh.

'But beyond that, Erica, there's not the slightest need to upset yourself.' Carol patted her arm with affectionate reassurance. 'After all, it was *you* that Oliver married. That's the really important point. She may be very glamorous and all that, but if it's you he loves, her whole box of tricks isn't worth very much, is it?'

'No, of course not.'

But Erica said her good-byes rather hastily after that. She suddenly wanted very much to get away before anything else was said, for, although Carol couldn't know it of course, it was that last remark which disturbed her more than anything else.

'If it's you he loves——'

So natural for Carol to say that. But it was like a stone thrown into the pool of her mind, making ever-widening circles of doubt and dismay. If it had been true, it *would* have been the strength of her position. But it was not true. And there was her weakness.

Erica walked part of the way home, because she wanted to think, and her mind went back for the thousandth time over the weeks of her honeymoon.

It had been nothing less than the truth when she had assured Carol that there had been no 'first quarrel.' Everything between them had been pleasant, easy-going and amicable. But, after the one unforgettable scene that night in Verona, he had seemed almost entirely withdrawn and remote again.

Erica had the queer impression that he was astounded and rather dismayed to find that he had been betrayed into anything so far removed from his usual unemotional ways. It hurt that he should faintly resent something which represented such happiness to her, but, with her understanding of him that amounted almost to instinct, she realised that only patience could serve her just now.

And so she had tried not to fret about it, but only to

think of the rare, sweet moments that might perhaps be hers.

'But it's very hard to be patient when all the time I'm afraid of every move that Dreda makes,' thought Erica, with a sigh, as she let herself into the big house.

And then Oliver came to the door of his study, with a curiously eager, 'Is that you, Erica?' And she realised with overpowering sweetness that, in his own way, he missed her when she was away.

She came over to him with a little smile. He didn't kiss her—he very seldom did—but he looked at her with a good deal of pleasure.

'I went to see Carol,' she explained. 'I thought it would be nice to surprise her the first day we were back.'

'Oh, yes!' He didn't even ask how Carol was, which was characteristic of him. Her surprise, or lack of it, evidently left him cold.

'Did you look in at the office?' she asked.

'Yes. Not for long. Just to see how things were.'

'And was everything all right?'

He shrugged.

'I miss my invaluable secretary already,' he told her with a smile.

'Oh——' Erica flushed. 'I'm sorry, Oliver.'

The smile deepened.

'I'm perfectly sure you're not. It's only human to be gratified at being proved indispensable.'

Erica laughed.

'I mean—I don't want you to be worried.'

'Why not?'

'Well of *course* not. I hate you to be troubled about things.'

'Funny child.' He took her by the chin in that abrupt but rather endearing way of his. 'I believe that's true. It is genuinely much more important to you that I should be spared worry than that your vanity should be pleasantly ministered to.'

She didn't know what to answer when he said this sort of thing. And after a moment she just said irrelevantly:

'I'm not a child.'

Whereat he laughed and drew her suddenly into the circle of his arm.

'No, I know you're not. It's the nicest thing about you—that you're grown-up and divinely sane and reliable. There, shall we have dinner now?' And, before she could even thank him for the compliment, he gently but firmly put her away from him.

But, for some reason, she didn't feel quite so frightened of Dreda, after all.

And in the end, Erica was there herself when the meeting between the two took place. It was not at the office, after all, nor at the house, but, quite casually, at a small party one evening.

Almost as soon as they had come home from their honeymoon, Erica had found Oliver prepared to take up a certain amount of social interests once more. After his accident, he had dropped them entirely until now, and Erica couldn't quite decide whether he had made the present change for her sake or because he had decided to make a complete break with the melancholy isolation of the last few years.

For her part, she was just a little nervous at first of having to play the rôle of a wealthy man's wife among her husband's own circle. But there was a certain innate sweetness and common sense about her that made people like her at once, and she immediately began to acquire a distinct popularity of her own.

'You're really just the right girl for Oliver to have married,' declared Cynthia Crome, who was considered by herself—and some others—to be more or less the leader of their set. 'I've known him—oh, for simply *years* now, and he used to be so gay and carefree before—well, before everything happened. Now that he has someone to sympathise with him and *understand* him, he'll probably be just like his old self again. There's such a lot in *understanding* men, isn't there?'

Erica murmured politely that there was, and secretly felt glad that Carol couldn't hear this touching effusion. She would undoubtedly have given an excellent burlesque of it on some awkward future occasion.

But Cynthia meant well, and, in her rather limp and artificial way, she was kind to Erica.

And it was at Cynthia's that Dreda chose to make her re-entry into Oliver's life.

There were about a dozen of them there already—the sort of party where almost anyone might drop in casually.

Erica was talking to Peter Crome, Cynthia's husband, and was not specially noticing any later arrivals, when suddenly there were exclamations of, 'Dreda! It's actually Dreda Canterley. My dear, we all wondered when you were going to notice our existence again.'

With an actual physical effort, Erica raised her head and looked across to the group by the door. And as she did so, she caught her breath a little. Dreda was so perfectly and frighteningly lovely. She wore an absolutely plain sheath-like dress of silver and from her hand there dangled carelessly a flaming chiffon handkerchief, the colour of her hair. That was all—just the two audacious notes of colour, but the effect was, to use Carol's word, stunning.

She came forward slowly, superbly sure that she was the centre of all interest. She was right—with one notable exception. Oliver, curiously enough, was unaware of her, as he stood by one of the windows, talking to Cynthia's father, with whom he was on excellent terms.

The old man was sitting on the window seat, and Oliver, his head slightly bent, had his back to the room.

It was all Erica could do not to go over and warn him, 'Dreda is here.' But of course it was impossible, and she could only watch Dreda's slow approach, knowing that Oliver was entirely unprepared.

'Well——' Dreda's touch on his shoulder was light, but he swung round at once. 'Are *you* going to ignore me, Oliver?'

Just for a second the barriers were down. Erica saw startled joy and then dismay and then—nothing. Oliver's face was a polite blank as he bowed over Dreda's hand.

But Erica found that she was trembling. She bit her lip until it bled—and hoped fervently that no one else had seen what she had seen.

She tried desperately to attend to the pleasant platitudes

which, with Peter Crome, constituted conversation, but it was dreadfully difficult.

And then Oliver raised his eyes and looked across the room at her.

Erica felt her heart turn over. There was nothing so definite as appeal in his look. Oliver would much rather have died than appeal to anyone, she knew. But she realised somehow that he wished she were there beside him.

She was perfectly calm in a moment, and, with a smile, she said to Peter :

'Why, there's Dreda Canterley. I must go over and speak to her. We only had about three minutes' talk on the day of our wedding, and then Oliver and I had to dash for the train, without even being able to apologise for the hurry.'

Peter nodded, and stood up at once. But his were not the only eyes that followed Erica across the room.

'Hello, Dreda.' Erica was a little surprised herself at her own calmness. 'We've been wondering when you would come in to see us. I expect you want to hear what we thought of Verona, don't you?'

This was carrying the war into the enemy's camp with a vengeance, and not only Dreda but Oliver too looked rather taken aback.

But Erica's smile was perfectly cool, as she slipped her arm into her husband's with an affectionately intimate little gesture. And then her composure gave rather, because she could feel that Oliver was very slightly trembling.

It was so utterly incongruous on anyone so hard and self-possessed as he that Erica wanted to throw her arms round him and cry. 'It's all right, darling. You mustn't mind so much about Dreda. She's little and mean and unimportant. You'll get over this madness, I *promise* you shall.'

But instead, of course, she had to keep up a smiling conversation, knowing all the time that Dreda's dangerous eyes were measuring her up afresh, while Dreda's good sense was telling her that, after all, this might be an adversary worthy of consideration.

And then Cynthia came up, some of the others drifted into the group, and the tension became much less.

Oliver quietly drew his arm away, and Erica found it hard to decide whether he had been grateful for her support or resentful that she should know of his need.

It was not until that difficult party was over, and they were at home once more and actually on their way up to bed, that she learned how he really had felt.

Instead of leaving her at the top of the stairs with his usual curt 'good night,' he took her hand in his.

'Thank you,' he said without even looking at her, but she knew what he meant.

'It's all right, Oliver.' She wanted to kiss him, but knew she must not overdo the scene. And so after a moment she just said quietly, 'Good night.'

'Must we say good night?' He spoke as quietly as she—so quietly that, for a moment, she scarcely knew what he meant.

Then her heart gave a great leap and she whispered, 'No, we need not—say good night.'

And she thought, as his fingers tightened on hers, that this was the strangest sequel possible to his meeting Dreda again.

During the next week or two Erica became increasingly aware that Oliver was happy at home, but distinctly the reverse at the office. He would come in with that grim air of suppressed irritation that she had known so well in his father's lifetime. And although it would disappear gradually during the evening, she was afraid the annoyance started all over again the next day.

'I suppose the new secretary *is* a bit of a failure,' she thought. And then, in all justice, 'But then, of course, Oliver isn't the easiest of employers.'

Finally she asked him outright: 'What is the new secretary like?'

'Rotten,' was the laconic reply. 'She's going at the end of the week.'

'Oh——' Erica looked slightly dismayed. 'What are you going to do then?'

'I really don't know.' Oliver frowned impatiently. 'I suppose there are other good secretaries to be found. I don't seem to have found them, that's all.'

'Oliver——'

'Yes?'

'Let me come back—just for a while—until you find someone else.'

'Nonsense.' He looked astonished. 'I couldn't have you doing such a thing.'

'Why not?'

'Well, it's ridiculous, now that you're my wife.'

'But I'd *like* to.'

He was silent for a moment, and she saw that, in spite of his emphatic refusal, he was sorely tempted to agree.

'Do let me. It needn't be for long. Just to get things straight again.'

'It seems so—odd.' He was more than half persuaded.

'But why? I worked there as your fiancée. Is being your wife so very different?'

'Well, don't you think so?' He gave her a dry little look. And at that she flushed deeply.

'Yes, of course. Only——'

'All right.' He gave in suddenly. 'It's very weak of me to let you, but I'll be unspeakably thankful to have you.'

And so it was arranged.

Erica was surprised to find how quickly she slipped back into the way of things, but there was a new intimacy in the atmosphere that blended very pleasantly with the old companionship.

He didn't say anything else about being glad to have her back, nor did he show any particular concern for her welfare. Until one evening, when they had been working late, both in his office. Suddenly he looked up and said :

'I shall have to stay a good while longer, but there's no reason why you should. You'd better go along home, Erica.'

'No, thank you.' She smiled a little to herself. It was amusing and rather intriguing to have him bother about how late she worked. At one time she could have gone on until she dropped, and he would scarcely have noticed, so long as there was still more work to be done.

'There's no need for you to wear yourself out,' he insisted obstinately.

'If you're working I can go on working too,' Erica assured him. 'It's what you've always expected your secretary to do.'

There was silence, and then he said with grim amusement:

'Are you reproaching me for slave-driving in the past?'

'No, of course not!' She glanced across at him for a startled second, but she dropped her eyes again almost at once. 'Marriage hasn't made me so helpless that I can't go on doing what I've always done, that's all,' she explained hastily.

He pushed back his chair, and came over to stand behind her.

'I did work you far too hard before, didn't I?'

'No.' She obstinately went on with her work and refused to look at him.

'Yes, I did. And for some reason, you didn't mind. I remember, you told me once that you liked working for me, and I believe it was true.'

'Of course it was.' She wished nervously that he would go back to his own seat and not stand so disturbingly near to her.

'Erica, look up at me.'

'No—why?' She could not quite hide her agitation.

'Because, my little secretary, I tell you to. And obedience is the first rule of a good secretary.'

'Oh——' She looked up then, reluctantly, and saw that even his eyes were smiling, a very rare thing with him.

'Would you really rather be working here with me than taking things easily at home?' he wanted to know.

'Why—why, yes,' Erica stammered slightly.

'You silly little idiot,' he said softly, but he leant forward and kissed her with sudden tenderness.

She didn't say anything—she scarcely knew what to say. And then he too straightened up without a word and went back to his own desk. But once or twice, when she glanced across at him later, she saw that he was still smiling faintly.

There was silence for some while between them, and then she heard him rummaging impatiently through some papers, jerking open a drawer or two, and pushing them

68

shut again with obvious annoyance.

'What is it, Oliver?' she said at last.

'That fool of a girl'—he was still looking round impatiently—'she contrived to put almost everything in its wrong place. You can't put your hand on that letter from Mervin & Gaskall, I suppose? The one about the long-term contract, you know.'

'Yes, I think so.' Erica got up and went over to the tall filing cabinet which stood by the window. He watched her, his annoyance slowly giving way to amusement.

'Here you are.' She picked out a file and brought it back to him.

He laughed outright then.

'You're unique, Erica.' He caught her hand lightly when she would have drawn back, and held her by his side for a moment. 'Um, you're quite right.' He glanced through the letter. 'This is what I wanted. How did you know what she'd done with it?'

'Well, she hadn't.' Erica smiled slightly. 'I found it straying about and filed it. That, Mr. Leyne, happens to be where that letter *should* be by now.'

'Then that's why it was the last place I thought of looking,' he said. 'She never put anything in its right place. Quite—unlike—you.' And for a brief moment he leant his head against her arm.

Erica glanced down at him with overwhelming tenderness. He was a little tired, she could see, but very well content to rest against her. And she thought what a long way they had come since his half mocking, half brutal proposal. Then she saw that he was actually using his gloved hand to turn over the papers in the file, and she knew he must be feeling completely at ease with her.

'There's the whole correspondence here, I suppose?' he said slowly. 'Didn't we have the first discussion of this deal when we were up at the house one evening? I seem to remember it. I made a note of the essential points then, I think. It should be here.'

She too remembered then, and she would rather have not. It had been the evening that Dreda's letter had come.

'Ah, here it is. And——'

He stopped. And, as he did so, Erica suddenly became rigid. For, caught up in the last papers in the file, was a grey envelope.

She knew what it was, even before he flicked it over to show the French stamp.

'Paris. The twentieth of September,' he read out, examining the post mark. 'Then——' He sprang to his feet suddenly, almost pushing her out of the way as he did so. 'Then Dreda's letter *did* come!'

She was absolutely silent. There was nothing at all she could think of to say. She could only hold her breath and watch in fascinated horror while he pulled the opened envelope apart—to find it empty.

'But where the devil is the letter? The envelope has been opened so——' Again he stopped. Then slowly he raised his heavy dark eyes to her face, with an expression she had never seen there before. 'The evening we had this file up at the house, *you* opened the post. I remember now. I was called away.'

She nodded, as though unable to help herself, and at that he came close to her again, and stared down at her with a dark, cold menace that terrified her.

'You—little—cheat,' he said slowly. 'Where is Dreda's letter?'

'Burnt,' whispered Erica.

'You *burnt* it? A letter to me—from Dreda!' He seized her wrist quickly and jerked her round towards him as she tried to turn away.

'No, no—not I. *You* burnt it,' she muttered stupidly.

'Stop being a little fool,' he said harshly. 'What do you mean?'

'It was there—on the desk—I'd crumpled it up. And then you—you used it to light your cigarette. I was speaking—on the telephone.'

'Do you mean to tell me you let me burn it? That you've known all this time that I destroyed the letter I'd been waiting for for years?' He held her so that she had to look at him, had to meet his cold, furious eyes.

'I—didn't—know,' she gasped.

'*What* didn't you know? Do you mean you didn't know

70

what was in the letter? Hadn't you read it?'

She tried to get away but he held her relentlessly.

'Had you read the letter?'

'No,' Erica lied desperately in panic, knowing the next moment how futile and idiotic that was.

There was a short silence, before he said drily:

'Then it is a little curious that you saw fit to crumple it up, surely?'

'Oh——' Erica stopped. 'Very well, then,' she cried with a kind of desperate defiance. 'I *had* read it.'

'Exactly. And being a jealous, deceitful little jade——'

'*Oliver!*'

But he went on as though she had not spoken. 'You decided to destroy it before I could see it.'

'I didn't! I tell you, I didn't. You burnt it yourself.'

'By your arrangement.'

'No.'

'Yes. You actually had the ironic audacity to arrange that *I* should think it worthless and so burn it. And by that, I suppose, you quieted your own miserable, lying conscience.'

'Oh, please—*please* don't talk to me like this.' Her voice was quivering, but she managed to keep back the tears. 'You must listen—I can explain.'

'Good God,' he said bitterly, 'can you actually think up something that will cover all the facts?'

'Oh, Oliver, listen——'

'I am listening.'

'I did read the letter. I did think for a moment that I would destroy it, and I crumpled it up instinctively. Then I realised what an awful thing I was doing——'

He laughed a little at that, but not with amusement.

'And—and I tried to smooth it out again. And before I could, the telephone rang. Then while I was answering it you came back, picked up the crumpled letter and lit your cigarette with it.'

'While you watched? That is the point—*While you watched.*'

At the expression on his face, she thought for an incredible moment that he was going to strike her. And then, because she had hated herself so much for lying before, and

71

because the resignation of despair was settling down on her, she faced him squarely.

'Very well then,' she said doggedly. 'Very well, I saw you do it.'

There was silence in the room for quite a minute. Then he said quietly:

'I could kill you—with the greatest of pleasure.'

'Oliver!' She shrank back as far as his grasp would let her.

'Only you're not worth doing time for.' And he almost pushed her away from him.

'But don't you understand—at all?'

'Yes,' he told her, 'I understand exactly. It's a very well told tale, which just may be true.'

'It *is* true.'

'Then in that case, you've merely shown yourself as a rotten little hypocrite as well as a cheat. You've split hairs for the sake of satisfying your own contemptible conscience, and you plead that because my hand, and not yours, destroyed the letter, it was not your fault.'

She was silent, because she saw how hopeless it all was. Then she winced afresh as he addressed her again in that cold, hard voice.

'And now we'll come to the crux of the matter. Just what did Dreda say in that letter?'

'Oh, Oliver—please! I can't tell you. It wasn't so very much, really——'

'Enough to make you destroy it,' he pointed out inexorably.

Erica was wretchedly silent again. And then he put his hand under her chin—not gently nor teasingly this time, but so that he jerked her face up and she had to meet his eyes.

'I think you'd better tell me what was in that letter,' he said quietly. 'Or I shall telephone Dreda and ask *her* to come here and tell me.'

Erica caught her breath on a sharp gasp.

'Oliver! You couldn't do anything so awful. So—so mean.'

He gave a short, contemptuous laugh.

'Are *you* accusing *me* of meanness? That's rather a dangerous line to take, you know, considering your own little excursion into letter-tampering.'

Erica winced.

'Suppose you tell me what was in that letter.' His voice was dangerously calm.

'She said'—Erica hesitated, and then went on desperately—'she said that she had often meant to write during the last few years, but had never quite been able to get up her courage.'

Erica saw his mouth tighten, but he only said:

'Go on.'

'She had just finished a concert tour and was having—was having several months in England before starting a new one.'

'Yes, yes.' He sounded violently impatient. 'Did she say anything about wanting to see me?'

Erica passed the tip of her tongue over her dry lips.

'She said—she would like to see you—that perhaps you would come to London unless——'

'Unless *what*?'

'Unless the past was too much past for it to matter any more.'

'God in heaven!' Oliver was very white. 'She said that? And you made me let the letter go unanswered?'

Just for a moment Erica's pride rose in revolt.

'You will remember, won't you,' she said with some dignity, 'that you were engaged to me at that time.'

'Engaged to you? That farce!' His careless, brutal anger silenced her. And then, as though recalling something, he said contemptuously: 'You wouldn't have lost by it.'

'What do you mean?'

'I would have paid you well—to go.'

'*Oliver!* How dare you? Are you mad that you can say these disgraceful things to me? I may have behaved badly over this letter—at least in your eyes. But I've done my best for you in every other way. I've—I've been loyal to you as a secretary and as a wife.'

And suddenly, as she remembered that dear tribute to her loyalty which he had made so long ago, she burst into frantic tears, and, sinking down at her desk again, buried her head on her arms.

He was silent for a moment or two, perhaps a little shaken by her tears.

Then he said rather coldly:

'I'm sorry if the reference to the money upsets you so much, but will you please remember, in your turn, that it was your reason for marrying me.'

'*No!*' She looked up then, very white.

'That was all I offered you—the material advantages which my wife might expect to enjoy.' His hard, dark eyes met hers challengingly. 'What else did you expect?'

'Oh——' She saw then that she was caught.

There was dead silence again. And then he said:

'You see? You're not in a very strong position.'

Erica looked away from him, out of the window, and wondered what was left of her world.

'Well,' she said at last, rather heavily, 'what do you propose to do?'

He made an impatient little movement, and turned away.

'God knows. I don't.' And he began to walk up and down the room with quick impatient steps.

She watched him helplessly. She felt there ought to be something she could do, something she could suggest. But her mind seemed a stupid blank.

At last he stopped in front of her.

'There isn't anything to do, of course,' he said harshly. 'You settled things very finally. We've got to go on living in the same house—hating each other.' Her nostrils quivered slightly, but she made no protest. 'I suppose we're not the only couple in the world doing that,' he added. 'And, later on, we can get a divorce quietly.'

She didn't say anything to that. She only asked one ridiculous, irrelevant question.

'Am I to go on being your secretary for the time?'

He looked astonished, and then laughed shortly.

'Do you *want* to?'

'Yes.' She didn't look at him. She thought, 'I haven't an atom of spirit. I'm just what Carol says—a doormat.'

'Why do you want to go on being my secretary? In order

74

to keep an eye on my correspondence?' he asked brutally.

'No. Only it won't be very nice, just sitting there at home in that great house with nothing to do but to—think.'

'I shouldn't imagine it would be exactly *nice* being my secretary, in the circumstances.' He spoke very drily.

'I'd rather have it that way,' she persisted.

'Very well, have it your way,' he exclaimed impatiently. 'But for heaven's sake go now. I don't feel I want to see you in the room any longer.' And he turned away with his back to her, and began to examine some papers with a nervous agitation he was powerless to hide.

She put on her outdoor coat, slipped quietly out of the room, closing the door behind her, and went downstairs and out into the street. It was quite dark, so no one could see how bitterly she was crying. In any case, of course, there was no one to care.

She walked home. It took a long time, but that was just as well, because she would have to present some sort of calm appearance to the servants when she got in.

As it was, the maid who met her in the hall said:

'Aren't you well, madam? You look so pale and tired.'

'I'm all right,' Erica told her. 'Just a little tired. I'll go straight up to my room. Is—is Mr. Leyne in yet?'

'Not yet, madam. Would you like anything in your room?'

'No, thank you.'

'Not even a cup of tea?' The girl was very much concerned, for all the staff liked Erica.

'No, thank you.' Erica smiled faintly and went upstairs. She thought how odd it was to be offered a cup of tea when your heart was broken. Once before, at least, disaster had touched her life—when she had lost both her parents and been left alone and stranded—but never before had she known this blank dismay, this certainty that nothing could ever be normal again. She felt that the ordinary, everyday things—eating, sleeping, going about the daily round—had become impossible, that something fantastic must surely take their place.

But she was quite wrong, of course. Nothing is so entirely relentless as the normality of everyday life. And Erica found, with a sort of aching relief, that if life didn't go on exactly as before, at least it went on.

Breakfast-time was almost the worst, she thought, when Oliver sat wordless behind his newspaper, and she pretended to be concerned with the small duties of the breakfast table. It seemed endless. Each bit of food seemed to stick in her throat, and she grew to hate the very smell of coffee. But after that it was not so bad. She took to going to the office rather earlier than he, and that avoided their going together. In the old days, she had always arrived at least half an hour before Oliver, so that it was not entirely illogical to do the same now.

During the day she worked almost all the time in her own room, although for a while after she had come back he had seemed to like to have her in his office. And then in the evenings they were very often out, and things were not so bad when other people were there.

But, even so, Erica began to look rather paler than nature had meant her to be, and her mouth was all the more startlingly red in contrast. Round her wide grey eyes, too, there were the faintest suggestions of shadow, and the next time she went to see Carol, there were some rather outspoken comments.

'What's he been doing to you? Beating you?' she wanted to know.

'No,' Erica said, and wished it had only been that.

'What then? I suppose you *have* had your first quarrel, after all, and it's been a beauty.'

'Don't!' Erica leant forward suddenly and put her face in her hands. She was not crying—she sometimes felt she had shed all the tears there were on that first evening—but she felt so tired and dispirited.

'Erica dear'—Carol's bantering tone changed entirely—'what *is* the matter? Is it that red-haired menace? But she's left the town, you know. You mustn't worry.'

'Has she?' Erica looked up. 'How do you know?'

'Oh, I'm not so simple as I look,' Carol assured her. 'I always make it my business to find out things when they're important.'

'Well, I don't know that it matters so very much,' Erica

said with a sigh.

'There, you see, I told you,' Carol exclaimed. 'If it's you he loves, what does the redhead matter?'

'It isn't,' Erica said starkly.

'What isn't?' Carol looked bewildered.

'It isn't me that he loves.' Erica pushed her hair back wearily and stared into the fire.

There was a moment's appalled silence, and then Carol came and sat on the rug at her feet. 'How do you know?' she asked at last in a dismayed whisper.

'He said so.'

'*He* said so?'

'Oh, we had it all quite clear from the beginning.' Erica suddenly didn't want to pretend any more. 'He—he had always loved Dreda, but she turned him down when he had that accident to his hand. He didn't really want anything but—well, I suppose companionship, from me. He told me he just *could* not love anyone else.'

'Do you mean he told you all this when he asked you to marry him?'

'Yes. He was perfectly straightforward about it.'

'Straightforward!' Carol gave a little snort of contempt. 'Well, Erica, if you don't mind my saying so, *I* think your husband is a prize cad.'

'Oh, no.' Erica put her arm lightly round Carol's shoulders. 'He had no idea my feelings were involved, you see. I'd been advising him to get married——'

'With yourself in view?' interrupted Carol with interest.

'*No*, of course not. Just that I was sure he would be happier married.'

'Darling, the matter with you is that you're altogether too idiotically disinterested,' Carol declared. 'If you thought about yourself a little more, and indulged in a little natural healthy selfishness you wouldn't get into these ghastly muddles. Still, go on.'

'Oh, I don't know really how we got involved in the discussion. Anyway, he more or less admitted he was wretchedly lonely, and of course his father was always pestering him to marry. And then, quite suddenly, he asked me, because he—he did like me then, you know.'

'Yes,' Carol admitted grudgingly. 'Even he shows a few glimmerings of taste at times. Well, he told you he couldn't love you, but if his bank balance would do instead, it was yours for the asking?'

Erica smiled faintly.

'Something like that.'

'And you were silly enough to take that on, feeling as you do? You know, dear, it was just plain lunacy,' Carol said regretfully.

'No!' Erica exclaimed with some energy. 'You don't know—things *were* working out all right. Oh, they were, Carol. And then Dreda wrote, just before we were married. It was a deliberate attempt to get him back, and she had been so awful to him—*awful*, in the old days. It would have been the same restless, miserable slavery as before. She had that effect on him.'

'And did you open the letter?'

'Yes. I was going through his post for him, and I found her letter.'

'Don't tell me you had the sense to destroy it?'

'Yes, I did. At least—no. I meant to. I crumpled it up. And then I saw what an awful thing it was to do. I was just smoothing it out again when the phone went. Then he came back, and used the crumpled piece of paper to light his cigarette. And I—I watched him do it.'

'Well?' Carol looked anxious. 'You weren't such a fool as to own up later, I suppose?'

'No—no. He found the envelope a little while ago. It had got caught up in a file.'

'Erica!' Carol looked exasperated. 'Really, dear, you are the most clumsy of criminals. If you did a murder you'd go and drop the gun at a policeman's feet.'

'I suppose so. I seem to make a mess of everything.' Erica sounded too dispirited to mind much what Carol said. 'But it was really my being deceitful in the beginning that started it. I had no right to do what I did about the letter. But I thought it was best—I honestly thought it was best. And even now'—she set her mouth with fresh determination—'even now, if I thought I'd saved him from Dreda, I—I wouldn't change things.'

'Well, I would,' Carol said with energy. 'I wouldn't have you looking pale and sad because some bounder of a man is fretting after some cat of a girl, if *I* could change it.'

'Don't, Carol dear.' Erica put her cheek against Carol's bright golden head. 'I can't bear to hear you talk like that about him. You make me sorry I told you, because it's only one side of Oliver. I can't tell you how dear he's been to me sometimes, and there *are* times when he struggles desperately against that angry moodiness of his, you know. Only it seems to him that I deliberately spoilt his chance of happiness. He—he says he'd waited years for a letter of hope from her. It's an awful thing to wait and wait for something that never comes.'

'Does he really think he'd be happier with that copper-headed Medusa than he would with you?' asked Carol grimly.

'I suppose so.'

'Then—I'm sorry—the man's a fool as well as everything else.'

Erica sighed. It was not possible that Carol would ever see Oliver with tolerant eyes. And Erica herself was too clear-sighted not to know that there was a certain amount of truth in what her friend said—which made it very difficult to argue.

Both girls were silent for a little while, and then Carol said: 'What are you going to do about it? Anything?'

'What is there I can do?' Erica looked sadly into the fire.

Carol muttered something which Erica took to be an outline of what *she* would have done in the circumstances, but she didn't press her to repeat it more plainly.

'Well, I suppose you will just go on as best you can, and hope that one day Oliver will wake up to the fact that he had a very lucky escape, and is extremely fortunate to be married to you.'

Erica moved slightly. She was thinking of what he had said about 'a quiet divorce later on.' But she could not bring herself to speak of that, even to Carol. So she said nothing, and after a moment Carol spoke, a little jerkily and without looking at Erica:

'There's just one thing——'

'Yes?'

'If ever things get—well, more than you can stand, and you feel you want to walk out on him, just do it, and come along to me here.'

'Carol!' Erica hugged her. 'You're the most generous girl alive, but I wouldn't think of it.'

'Why ever not?' Carol sounded deliberately matter-of-fact. 'The flat's here. Your old room wouldn't take much getting ready. And if you were a little while getting another job, what's the odds? I may be improvident, but I do keep a moth-eaten little nest egg for emergencies. Not that moths eat eggs, of course,' she added in parenthesis as Erica kissed her.

'You are absurd and sweet,' Erica told her with tears in her eyes. 'And you're specially absurd and sweet when you're trying to pretend you have a flinty heart.'

Carol laughed a little.

'I *am* hard-hearted,' she declared. But Erica would have none of it. And afterwards, when she was going home, she remembered suddenly the time she had defended Carol sharply to Oliver, and she felt quite extraordinarily glad of it.

It was about a week after this that they were at Cynthia's again one evening, and Colin Lamb was there. It was the first time Erica had seen him since her wedding, although she had known that he was in England, and she was touched and pleased at the friendly way he greeted her.

'Do come and talk to me,' he said, smiling down at her from his considerable height. 'I feel I ought to know Oliver's wife very well, but one marriage service and a hasty luncheon afterwards scarcely constitute much of an acquaintance.'

Erica smiled in return, and came very willingly to sit with him in the rather secluded corner he had indicated.

'Have you been very busy with your concerts?' she asked shyly, because, she thought, men usually had a weakness for themselves as a topic of conversation.

Colin Lamb, however, seemed a determined exception. 'But I didn't mean that we should talk about me,' he said, still smiling a little. 'I thought we were going to talk about you.'

'Couldn't we talk about both of us?' suggested Erica demurely, to hide the fact that she was nervous of any discussion about herself.

He laughed outright then.

'I suppose we could. And in that case, I must give you the choice of topic, and so we *will* start with me. Thank you—I've been very busy with concert arrangements, and now I'm very glad to be having a bit of a holiday.'

'And will you please tell me what sort of concerts they are?' Erica said earnestly. 'I know I must sound dreadfully ignorant, but, beyond the fact that you said something about chamber music, and that it was through that you met Oliver, I honestly don't know anything much about you.'

Colin didn't seem at all piqued, however, only slightly amused.

'There's no real reason why you should,' he assured her. 'I happen to belong to a string quartet of moderate fame. We're very well known on the Continent, and passably well known here. I play first violin.'

'You are the leader, in fact?'

'Well, yes,' he admitted, again with the smile which Erica found singularly charming.

'And are the others English?'

'Oh, no. One Norwegian and two Austrian, but we get on extremely well. It was in our very early days, before we well known at all, that we used to see a good deal of Oliver,' he explained.

'You mean you used to play together?' Erica was suddenly intensely interested in this side of Oliver's life.

'Yes. I suppose you know that Oliver was a very fine pianist before he hurt his hand?' Colin looked at her enquiringly.

'I—I rather gathered so. At least, he told me once how much it meant to him——' She stopped and bit her lip. The scene in the bedroom in Verona had suddenly come back with almost unbearable clearness. He had been so much hers then—so much. And now it was all spoilt.

But if Colin noticed the hesitation he made no sign of

having done so.

'Oliver really was a wonderful player,' he said thoughtfully. 'Not much more than a very brilliant amateur at that age of course, but he would have developed into a concert professional without any doubt. And his whole heart and soul were in it.' Colin's slightly cynical mouth softened very kindly. 'I simply cannot imagine what a tragedy it must have been for him, that accident. It was like striking a brilliant speaker dumb.'

Erica's eyes widened. She wished suddenly that she could have known Oliver then, known him before his despairing isolation had hardened him. It would have been so much easier to have comforted him then, so much easier to have *reached* him.

'And then, of course, there was losing Dreda too,' she said very gently—rather more to herself than to Lamb.

He looked at her sharply.

'You know about that, too, then?' he said.

'Oh, yes.'

There was silence for a moment, and then he said slowly:

'I'm not telling you this with the idea of gratifying you, but, actually, Mrs. Leyne, it was no tragedy for Oliver to lose Dreda Canterley.'

'No?' Erica's grave eyes came back to his face once more. 'I wonder just what you mean by that?'

He didn't answer at once.

'Did you know Dreda at all?' he asked at last.

'Only a little. And I don't think I look at her with entirely unprejudiced eyes,' Erica told him with a faint smile.

'It's generous of you to admit it. Most people would blind themselves to that—rather naturally,' Colin said. 'But I think I can speak with a fair lack of prejudice, and I can only say that I would not wish any friend of mine—least of all one with Oliver's defenceless nature—a lifetime with Dreda.'

'That's a strange word to use of Oliver,' Erica said with a thoughtful expression. 'It's quite true, of course. He *is* most peculiarly defenceless, though most people would think it an extraordinary way of describing him.'

'Well, I suppose you and I both know him very well, and are both very fond of him. And that's why we see the same thing,' Colin said. 'For, in spite of all his faults—and I'm sure you know as well as I that he has them—I *am* tremendously fond of him.'

'I know you are.' Erica smiled at him. 'I think that's why I liked you at once.'

He acknowledged that with an answering smile.

'You know the liking was mutual, don't you?'

'I hoped so,' Erica said quite simply.

'I don't mind admitting that I was unspeakably glad when I saw the type of girl Oliver had chosen. To be quite candid, I hadn't credited him with quite such acute judgment.' And Colin laughed slightly.

'Because he made a bad slip over Dreda, you mean?'

'I suppose so.'

'But she's so brilliant and dazzling that lots of men would lose their heads over her,' Erica said honestly.

'Perhaps that's it.' Colin's expression somehow suggested that his own head had never been in any danger. 'Her playing is just the same, you know.'

'Is it? Is she a pianist, too?'

'Yes. An incredibly brilliant technician. And one is, as you say, quite dazzled for the time.'

'And behind it all?'

He laughed. 'A soul as shallow as that,' he said, measuring a tiny space between his thumb and finger.

'Oh.' Erica didn't laugh. She was perfectly serious. And then Cynthia came over to break up the conversation with the declaration that they had hidden themselves away quite long enough. But somehow, during the remainder of the evening, Erica thought very often of that last remark of Colin Lamb's.

Even on the way home, she glanced once at Oliver's rather grim profile and thought:

'In a way, it *was* like rescuing him.'

And when they got home there was a letter for him from Dreda. It was lying on the top of the pile of letters which had been left on a table in the library. It was impossible for Erica not to see it. She felt that her eyes were riveted to

83

it—and then she raised them slowly and met his.

Without a word, he picked up the pile of letters and sorted them rapidly. There were a couple for her, which he handed to her. Unimportant letters which she opened absently and read again and again without taking in the sense.

She knew he was reading his. Business letters. Conventional social letters. And Dreda's letter.

She felt she ought to go. It was ridiculous and undignified to linger like this. And yet she could not drag herself away.

'Oliver,' she said at last, and her voice was strained and a little high-pitched because she was so nervous.

'Yes?'

'I—I'm going to have a hot drink. It was so dreadfully cold driving home. Would you like one, too?'

'I should think all the servants are in bed,' he said indifferently.

'It doesn't matter. I'll make it.'

'Will you?' He did look up then. 'Thanks. I should like one if you're getting it anyway.'

She put off her little white fur coat without a word and went out of the room.

When the drink was ready she carried it back into the library. He was sitting down now, staring into the fire, but he rose at once when she came in, and took the tray from her.

Erica sat down, rather because she felt unable to stand any longer. But he stood on the hearthrug, towering above her and making her feel very much at a disadvantage.

It was difficult to think of anything to say. There *was* nothing to say. And the heavy silence went on, unbroken.

Only when at last she got up with a murmured 'good night,' he said:

'Erica.'

'Yes.' With an effort she raised her eyes to his, and saw that he was not entirely at ease either.

'I think I'd better tell you. I'm going to London next week-end.'

'To see Dreda?' It was out, in all its nakedness, before she could stop it.

There was a cold silence.

'Dreda is giving a concert,' he said at last. 'And—yes, I shall be going.'

'Concert?' Erica gave a sad little laugh.

'What do you mean by that?' He turned on her fiercely. 'Are you suggesting——'

'I'm not suggesting anything,' she said quietly. 'I—just wish you wouldn't go, that's all.'

Up went his eyebrows. 'Are you standing up for your wifely rights or something?' he asked her sarcastically.

'I wasn't thinking of myself,' Erica said simply.

'How disinterested of you. Of whom were you thinking? Of me?'

'Yes.'

'But why think of me rather than you?' He was smiling drily, she knew, from the tone of his voice. And suddenly she raised her head and looked full at him with those grave eyes of hers.

'Because it isn't my soul that's in danger, Oliver,' she said quietly, 'It's yours.'

He looked exceedingly taken aback, and it was a moment before he answered.

'Are you objecting on some moral ground?' he said at last.

'Oh, no.' She shook her head. 'I'm not suggesting you'd start an affair with Dreda. That isn't what she wants at all. It's something quite different.'

'What then?' She saw that he was curiously shaken.

Erica put her hands very lightly on his arms and looked up at him.

'You don't really think that Dreda brings out the best in you, do you?' she said quietly.

His eyes widened a little.

'Exactly what do you mean by that?' he asked curtly.

It was difficult to go on, but she *had* to.

'There's a terribly hard streak in you, Oliver,' she said sadly, 'and it's to that that she inevitably appeals. I don't quite know whether it's natural to you or—or whether circumstances have put it there, but there *is* that hardness, and everything she demands of you increases it.'

She stopped, but he didn't say anything. He just stared moodily down at her.

'I'm sorry——' She moved her hand nervously on his arm. 'But it—it was something that had to be said.'

'So you think I'm hard?' He still didn't move.

'In some ways—yes.'

'And what are you?'

She smiled slightly at that.

'Lots of regrettable things, I don't doubt, but I don't think hardness is one of them. I'm rather the other way, I suppose—soft enough to be a little bit of a fool.'

'So you think it's a sign of softness to be able to marry a man just because he has money?'

'I—didn't.' She whitened a little.

'Didn't what? Didn't marry me for my money?'

'No.' It was quiet but distinct.

'Indeed. Then what *was* your reason for marrying me?' he asked drily.

And at that she drew a quick breath, and looked at him with a little touch of pride.

'I married you for one reason—and one reason only, Oliver. Because I love you.'

CHAPTER IV

'WHAT—did you—say?'

He stepped back sharply and stood there staring at her, his anger slowly giving way to a sort of incredulous dismay.

She didn't repeat what she had said. She too stood there waiting, wondering a little which of them would be forced to break the silence first. For her part, she knew of nothing she could say. That one stupendous confession had wiped any other thought from her mind.

'But I told you'—his voice was slightly hoarse—'I told you from the beginning that I wanted none of that.'

She did move then, and found her voice:

'One doesn't always wait to be asked for—one's love, Oliver. Sometimes it's given quite freely from the beginning.'

'Do you mean——' He stopped, and then went on in a low voice, as though he would willingly have been silent but could not. 'When did you first love me?'

'Always, I think,' Erica told him quietly.

'Oh, *no*!' He turned away quickly, with a little of awe as well as anger on his face.

'You mustn't mind so much.' She put her hand on his shoulder, even smiling a very little at his odd dismay.

'But I don't want it. I have no use for it.' He spoke jerkily.

'You don't have to do anything about it, Oliver.' She thought it queer that she was almost reassuring him. 'You can forget it now. Only don't—ever—accuse me again of marrying you for your money.'

'I won't,' he said in a very low voice, and, taking her hand in his suddenly, he kissed it. 'I'm sorry—for some things, you know. I just didn't realise.'

'Didn't you?' She looked at his bent head very tenderly. 'I used to think you must surely know. I imagined I gave myself away quite often.'

'No.' He was playing with her fingers a little nervously, without knowing that he did it. 'I never thought about it at all. I just knew that I was ha——' He stopped.

The unspoken word seemed to hang there between them in the silence, but he obstinately refused to give it utterance.

He let go her fingers and thrust his hand down into his pocket. She saw a slight change come over his face, and he drew out Dreda's letter. There was silence for a moment, and then, slowly, he raised his heavy eyes to hers. She held her breath, and, just for a second, hope struggled desperately in her heart.

But when he spoke, his voice was cold and without any shadow of indecision now.

'I'm sorry,' he said deliberately, 'but this doesn't make any real difference, you know.'

Her lips moved, but no words came. She couldn't plead that because she loved him he must surely pity her and try to love her, too. That wasn't what she meant in any case. She had not been offering her love as a bribe, she thought, wincing. It was only that, since the words had been forced from her, she had had some faint hope they might make a difference.

Well, she had been wrong, that was all.

She had lost.

The fact that she loved him could not really weigh against the fact that he loved Dreda. Why should it?

Without a word, she picked up her coat absently, put it over her arm, and went slowly out of the room. It would have been absurd to say good night again after all that had happened.

He said nothing either. But he followed her with his eyes until the door closed quietly behind her.

In the next few days it seemed to Erica that the atmosphere between them changed a little. It was not that he was any kinder to her, or that, even in the office, he showed her any special consideration. But there was no more of that subtle, perpetual suggestion of contempt. She might almost just have been his efficient secretary once more—outside his private feelings entirely, but with a certain impersonal worth in his official life.

She wondered a little if he were deliberately creating that impression in his own mind, to escape the feeling that he was wronging her by every thought he gave to Dreda.

And then, in the middle of the week, she happened to hear him say to someone on the telephone:

'I'm not sure I shall be here at the week-end. I'll let you know for certain later. What? No, I'm sorry, I really don't know myself, at the moment——'

She didn't wait to hear any more. She slipped back into her own room and sat at her desk with the most ridiculous hope stirring in her heart.

He had *not* decided yet. There was still a chance that he might refuse Dreda's request. That had been no business prevarication, she knew. If he had been certain he was going away, he would just have said so.

It was the slenderest thread to cling to. No one who was not very foolish—or very desperate—would have clutched at it. But it was there.

He might not go.

Erica guessed where Dreda had made the mistake. She had gone away—left the town. At one time, absence had been a very strong weapon, because he had had nothing but his flaming, agitated thoughts to keep him company.

But now it was her actual physical presence that had its effect on him. When she went, there *was* something to take her place. The great empty, melancholy house was empty and melancholy no longer.

'Oh, God, if only you'll keep her away,' muttered Erica, putting her head in her hands. 'He doesn't love me. He never would now, of course. I don't ask that. But if only she'd stay away, I think I might break the chain in time.'

She scarcely realised how high her hopes had grown on the strength of that one sentence on the telephone. Until they were dashed to the ground once more by the sight of Dreda's famous scarlet and cream car streaking through the town.

Erica had been coming through the shopping district on her way home, because there was something she had wanted to buy, but at the sight of that car every thought of shopping was wiped from her mind.

Actual physical fear clutched at her heart, and she felt her very cheeks go cold. What on earth was Dreda doing here—miles away from London—only a day or two before her concert?

It must be something very important to have brought her all this way. And, in her eyes, there was only one important thing here—Oliver.

'It's no good. I can't fight any more,' Erica thought wildly. And then: 'But I will fight. I *will*. What's the good of any love if it won't fight for existence?'

She walked quickly through the streets, not looking in shop windows any more, threading her way through the crowds. Physically, she felt intensely tired—because of the shock, she supposed. But her mind was tremendously alert, wide awake, searching for some way out of this tangle.

And then, quite suddenly, she saw what it was that she must do. She must go and see Dreda herself.

She had scarcely an idea of what she would say, but the moment would give her inspiration. They could not go on like this, pretending that everything was perfectly all right, when in reality everything was all wrong.

Even the Dredas of this world must understand *some* form of appeal. She must have loved Oliver once, in her way. Well, perhaps 'love' was not quite the word. But at any rate she must have had kindly feelings for him—wished him to be happy. She *must* understand now that she was ruining everything, in her slow destruction of his peace of mind.

With a perfectly steady hand, Erica hailed a taxi. She was astonished to find how calm she was. But in moments of crisis one must be calm. It was the one faint chance of success.

She had never been to Dreda's home before, of course, but she knew it quite well from the outside. A pleasant, elegant place of moderate size, set in most beautiful grounds. Dreda's parents had lived there for many years, and although her father had been dead some while, her mother still kept on the house, mostly because her lovely, imperious daughter demanded that there should always be a permanent home for her somewhere.

That she practically never visited the permanent home apparently had nothing to do with it. Mrs. Canterley was too much under Dreda's domination to rebel on a point like that. A pretty, faded, rather ineffectual woman, she believed that the world revolved round her brilliant daughter. And her brilliant daughter did nothing to disabuse her of the notion.

Evidently Dreda had scarcely more than arrived, because the maid who opened the door seemed surprised that Erica should know she was at home.

'I saw Miss Canterley's car in town,' Erica explained, 'and I should very much like to speak to her for a moment if she will see me.'

The maid murmured that she would find out if Miss Canterley were free, and went away, leaving Erica to look round the long, beautiful room, and to hope that Dreda would not leave her long enough for her nervousness to get the better of her once more.

But perhaps Dreda's curiosity got a little the better of *her*, because she came in almost at once. She was in a moss green suit, which did wonderful things to the lights in her red hair, and over it she still wore her white leather motoring coat.

She didn't offer Erica her hand. Her own were thrust into the pockets of her coat, as she came forward, smiling and very faintly insolent.

'Why, Erica, what is it? You don't mind if I call you Erica, do you? "Mrs. Leyne" seems so ridiculously formal.'

'I never remember her calling me Mrs. Leyne, in any case,' thought Erica. But aloud she only said, 'No, I don't really mind what you call me.'

'Oh——' Dreda laughed, 'you're offering almost too wide a scope now. But won't you sit down? Cigarette?'

Erica sat down, but she refused the cigarette.

Dreda lit one herself, and leant back completely at her ease.

'Did you come to see me about something special?' she asked nonchalantly. 'Or is this just a—friendly visit?'

'No,' Erica said slowly, 'it's not a friendly visit.' And

91

then, because there was no special way of wrapping up the crude fact, 'It's about Oliver.'

'Oliver!' Up went Dreda's finely marked eyebrows. 'But don't you think that Oliver is very well able to look after himself?'

'Oh, no.' Even at that moment Erica smiled faintly and rather tenderly. 'Oliver isn't in the least able to look after himself. That's why you managed to get such a tremendous ascendancy over him.'

There was a stunned silence. The very quietness of Erica's voice added to the force of the remark, and Dreda's nostrils quivered a little as she deliberately stubbed out her cigarette and watched the last of the smoke rising, before she answered.

'Are you trying to tell me that you resent the fact that your husband loves me?' she said at last, delivering her counter-blow with a coolness that at least equalled Erica's.

Erica winced. It was quite impossible not to. And then she said, quite steadily:

'I resent the fact that you're trying to take away my husband from me. Any woman would.'

'Sorry.' The faintest scornful smile just touched Dreda's mouth. 'But the brutal fact is that he wasn't ever yours, you know, so there's no question of taking him away.'

'He's my husband,' Erica said quietly.

Dreda shrugged.

'What is there in that? Any girl can make a man put a ring on her finger. The point is—what does it mean when it's there?'

Erica put her hand quickly round her little thin gold ring, rather as though she would protect it against Dreda's sneers.

'*My* ring means that Oliver put it there in the hope that he and I should find a certain peace and dignity and happiness together.' Her voice quivered very slightly, but she went on steadily: 'We *were* finding it. We *were* happy. But you're doing your best to spoil it all.'

'My dear girl, I can't very well help it if Oliver finds me more attractive than you.' There was a sort of amused exasperation in Dreda's tone, but her eyes were very hard.

'You know that you're just shirking the question, don't you?' Erica said rather sadly. 'That you're raising hollow excuses because you can't deny what I'm saying.'

'Really, I'm afraid I don't feel the miserable sinner that you seem to think I should,' Dreda declared lightly.

'I'm not trying to make you feel anything of the sort,' Erica told her patiently. 'I'm not asking you to own up to anything. Why should I? It's not my business. All I am asking is that you leave him alone in future—that you give me my rightful chance to make him happy.'

'It sounds terribly solemn to me.' Dreda laughed a little. 'But just what have I done to bring down these heroics on my head?'

'You asked him to come to London to see you, didn't you?' Erica's voice was quiet and entirely without rancour, but somehow it was not very easy to meet her eyes.

'Oh, that's what's piqued you, is it?' Dreda gave a contemptuous little toss of her head. 'But he *wants* to come, you know.'

Erica said nothing. She just went on looking at Dreda. And after a moment Dreda said carelessly:

'Well, I'll tell him *not* to come, if that's what all the fuss is about.' But she smiled to herself with a touch of wickedness that Erica could not mistake.

'You mean you'll put your refusal in such a way that any man would be provoked into coming?' she said.

'Really, you're very difficult to please,' exclaimed Dreda. 'I can't do more than tell him not to come, can I? Even anyone as possessive and resentful as you must see that.'

Erica took that without wincing. It was scarcely worth noticing in its spitefulness, she thought.

'Dreda,' she said almost gently, 'don't you *care* whether Oliver is happy or not? You must have some sort of feeling for him or you wouldn't bother about him like this. You must hate the fact that he has suffered so much and wish that he could find some sort of peace and happiness. You *must*!'

Dreda raised her eyes and looked across curiously at Erica. And at their expression Erica almost shrank back.

She saw suddenly, with a sense of utter futility, that

Dreda did *not* care in the very least. Oliver had no significance for her at all beyond the fact that he could minister to her senses and her vanity. She scarcely even looked cruel. She just looked blank. Erica might as well have been talking a foreign language for all the meaning that reached her.

It was no good. Erica saw that now. She had humiliated herself for nothing, because Dreda neither knew nor cared what ruin she caused.

Sick and dispirited and weary almost beyond endurance, Erica got unsteadily to her feet.

'I think I'd better go,' she said huskily.

'I think perhaps you had,' agreed Dreda calmly.

And at that moment the door opened, and the maid announced in her correct, rather precise tones:

'Mr. Leyne.'

Both girls gave something of a gasp as he came into the room. It was a *contretemps* neither of them had thought of.

But if they were surprised, Oliver was staggered. He didn't even bother to greet Dreda before he said sharply:

'Erica! What on earth are you doing here?'

Anyone but Oliver would have covered it up better than that, of course, and Dreda gave an amused little grimace before she said:

'Really, Oliver, isn't your wife allowed to pay me a visit without your permission?'

Oliver looked a little taken aback himself to find he had said anything so crude, and for a moment Erica thought that Dreda's coolness had saved the situation. But apparently Dreda didn't specially want the situation to be saved. For she added almost immediately:

'We had something very important to discuss.' And she smiled at Oliver in that provoking way of hers.

'Indeed? Am I permitted to ask what?' Oliver didn't seem specially pleased even with Dreda.

'Certainly, since it concerns you, too,' Dreda told him coolly. 'We were discussing the best way of making you happy.'

'The—*what*?' Oliver's face went dark, but Dreda was

94

quite unperturbed.

'Yes. You see, Erica thinks I'm ruining your happiness.'

'Dreda!' The faint exclamation came from Erica. But Oliver turned on her in undisguised fury.

'What in heaven's name do you think you're doing?'

Erica stared at him in wordless dismay.

'Come, you mustn't speak to her like that,' Dreda said lightly. 'She's perfectly entitled to her views, you know, even if they don't coincide with—ours. Erica and I have had a nice little chat, and since she feels rather sore about your coming to my concert, perhaps you'd better not come.'

Oliver went over to where Erica was standing.

'Have you dared——' He stopped suddenly and obviously controlled his temper with a great effort. 'I really don't think there's any point in our continuing this discussion here,' he said more quietly, to Dreda. 'As Erica was evidently just going home, I'll take her with me now. I really only dropped in to say that I *shall* be at the concert on Saturday evening.'

'*Will* you? But is it wise?' murmured Dreda.

Oliver gave her a black look, which had intense misery behind it too.

'I shall come,' he said curtly. 'Shall we go now, Erica?'

They went.

Not a word was said between them in the car on the way home. It was not until they were in their own house that the storm broke. He turned to her in the hall and said very quietly:

'Will you come into the library, please. There's something I want to say to you, and it can't be said here.'

He held open the door, and, feeling like a condemned criminal, she went slowly in.

He closed the door and leant against it, while Erica sank down into a chair because she could not possibly stand any longer.

'Now will you please tell me exactly what you were doing at Dreda's?'

'No.'

Erica, as well as Oliver, was astonished that there was such a simple answer to the question.

'But you've *got* to answer me.' He came forward and towered over her. 'You don't suppose you can go interfering in my private affairs and then flatly refuse to tell me what you were doing.'

'Is Dreda one of your private affairs?' Erica could not entirely keep the bitterness out of her voice, and he looked taken aback for a minute. But he recovered almost at once.

'Will you tell me what you were doing there?'

But suddenly Erica's control broke. She sprang to her feet and faced him.

'No, I will *not* tell you! I will not be hounded and bullied and lectured in this ridiculous way. You seem to think that because I'm living in your house every thought and action of mine is subject to your scrutiny. You used to talk of your father trying to live your life for you. You're ten times worse yourself——'

She paused for a moment at the expression of startled dismay that crossed his face, but, for the first time in her life, burning anger had overwhelmed her, and she was quite powerless to stop the rush of furious words that rose to her lips.

'You treat me like some—some animal who must wait on your pleasure. If you choose to ignore me, then I must put up with it. And if you choose to crush me with your— pompous displeasure, I must put up with that too. You made an abominable bargain with me in the beginning— yes, I know I was fool enough to accept it, and so, in a way, it was my own fault—but your air of virtuous indignation if I don't keep to every miserable letter of it is outrageous!'

She stopped once more, rather more for want of breath than anything else, and she saw then how very much shaken he was by what she had said. If the hearthrug had risen up and addressed him he could scarcely have been more surprised. But even then he refused to capitulate.

'And it was in order to confide all this in her that you went to see Dreda?' he asked drily, though his voice was not entirely steady.

'No, it was not. It was to ask her to stop trying to steal my husband—just as any woman would to to any man-catching bitch and try to—to spike her guns.'

'Erica!' Just for a second she saw something faintly like amusement struggling with his anger. And then suddenly the full impact of what she had said seemed to reach him. 'You went to Dreda and talked me over like that? Haggled over me as thought I were something in a shop?'

'Well, no, not just like that.' The fire was going out of Erica, and she felt that deadly weariness pressing on her again.

'How dared you do such a thing?' And then perhaps remembering her outburst against him and the horrid word 'pompous,' he spoke much more calmly. 'Can't you see that any man would loathe the whole idea?'

'Yes. I'm sorry,' she said quietly. 'You weren't intended to know anything about it, of course. It's one of those situations that are permissible if they remain private and quite unpardonable if not.'

'You can't dismiss it entirely like that.' He spoke coldly and with perfect self-control now, but she could see how angry he still was.

'What do you expect me to do? Grovel?'

'No, of course not,' he said stiffly. 'I merely want you to understand, once and for all, that you have no right of any sort to interfere in my private affairs. Even if our marriage were an ordinary one I should bitterly resent your going and—scrapping with some other woman about me, because you didn't happen to like my going to some public function where she would be. But, as things are, it's unendurable.'

'A lot of things are unendurable,' murmured Erica, but he took no notice of that.

'I'm sorry if you're dissatisfied with the bargain we made, but I have no intention of changing it now.'

'You mean you reserve the right to do what you please with any woman, without allowing me even a protest?' Erica said drily.

'My dear Erica, if you're concerning yourself with moral charges, you can set your mind at rest now,' he retorted shortly. 'I'm not at all the man of *affaires* that you seem anxious to imply.'

'There are other ways of being unfaithful besides spending the night with a woman,' said Erica, surprised at her own crude frankness.

Perhaps he was surprised too. At any rate, there was silence for a moment. Then he said obstinately:

'Well, where do we stand now?'

'What do you mean?' She pushed back her hair wearily and looked at him in some astonishment.

'Do I understand that in future you will allow me to look after my own private affairs?' he asked. And then, as though he didn't quite like the expression after all, he corrected it to 'my own private business.'

'Yes,' she said slowly, and there was a resignation in her voice that was beyond even bitterness. 'I will never attempt to touch your private life again. Never. Unless you ask me to yourself.'

'Erica!' he said in surprise at her curious way of putting it. But she didn't pause even to look at him. She turned and went out of the room without another word.

As she went slowly up to her room she felt that the only thing in the world she wanted was to go and lie on her bed and rest. But as soon as she was lying there—in the dark because she could not bear the thought of light on her misery—she found it was impossible to rest after all.

What had she ever done that life should treat her in this frightful way? she wondered. Some people said that foolishness was punished even more heavily than wickedness, and if that were so, perhaps she was paying for the utter foolishness of marrying Oliver when she had known he didn't love her.

It had been foolish, of course. 'Just plain lunacy,' Carol had called it.

And then, at the thought of Carol, she gave a great sob of relief. She must go there. She *must* be comforted by Carol with her dear uncritical affection and her sturdy common sense.

Oh, if only it were not too late in the evening to go!

With trembling fingers, she fumbled for the switch, and put on the light. Then she stared at the little silver clock in stupefaction. It couldn't possibly be as early as that. Only eight o'clock still!

She turned her wrist quickly and looked at her watch—

the little diamond watch that Oliver had given her, and which she always wore, day and night.

It, too, said eight o'clock.

Erica put her hand against her aching forehead. It seemed beyond belief. Both those awful, appalling scenes had been crammed into less than two hours.

Oh, well, it didn't matter now. The really important thing was that there was still time to go and see Carol.

If only she didn't feel so cruelly tired. But she mustn't think about that.

Rather feebly she put on her outdoor things and went quietly downstairs. No one was about, for which she was profoundly thankful, but even then she didn't like to wait while she phoned for a taxi. She must chance picking one up fairly quickly.

She went quite a long way, however, before she found one, and then she almost fell into it. But it covered the distance to the flat very quickly, and the thought of seeing Carol helped to buoy her up.

'My dear!' Carol's first exclamation was one of sheer pleasure. And then, as the light fell on Erica's face, she said, 'My dear!' again, but in a quite different tone.

Erica didn't say anything at all. She just let Carol lead her into the little sitting-room and put her into a chair by the fire.

Carol switched off the overhead light, leaving just the glow of a standard lamp. Then she brought in some brandy and made her drink it in spite of her rather vague protests.

'Feeling better now?' Carol sat down on the arm of Erica's chair and put her arm around her.

'Yes, thank you, much better. I—I got very cold coming here, you know.'

'Yes, I know,' was all Carol said.

There was a long silence, and then Erica said quietly:

'There's been—the most awful—scene.'

'With Oliver?'

'Well, with Dreda first, and—and then with Oliver.'

'With Dreda?' Carol looked a little disturbed.

'Yes, but that scarcely matters. It was quite useless, anyway. We can just—wash it out.' Erica drew a deep sigh and leant her head against Carol.

Carol looked at her very affectionately, but forbore to ask any questions, and presently Erica went on:

'Oliver found me there. And afterwards, when we got home, he was furious and then—so was I. I said the most dreadful things to him. It's just like looking back on delirium.'

'*You* said dreadful things to Oliver!' exclaimed Carol. 'I don't believe it. It's too good to be true.'

'Oh, no.' Erica shook her head slowly. 'I told him he was cruel and unreasonable and—and pompous, and ten times worse than his father.'

'You *what*? Oh, I wish I'd been there,' said Carol fervently.

'Why, Carol? It wasn't very nice,' Erica said wearily.

'No?' Carol looked grimly amused. 'But I'd have given a great deal to see his face when the worm turned and he found it was a boa-constrictor, after all.'

Erica laughed very faintly. And then, as though something had been unlocked by that very human sound, she suddenly began to cry, in deep, heart-rending sobs that seemed to shake Carol as much as herself.

'Erica, don't! You simply mustn't, dear. This must be frightfully bad for you.' Carol tried desperately to soothe her. 'He isn't worth it—really, he isn't. No man is.'

'I was crazy—I was crazy ever to take it on,' gasped Erica, between her sobs.

'Yes, I know, darling. But don't start reproaching yourself now. And please, please don't cry so,' begged Carol.

After a while Erica seemed to hear her appeals. The wild weeping stopped, and she lay back in her chair, terribly pale and quiet, but looking much less strained.

For quite a long while Carol said no more to her, only smoothing her hair affectionately as though she were a child. Then at last she said in a most matter-of-fact tone:

'I'm going to get supper now. You'll have some, too, won't you?'

Erica began to say no, that she wasn't hungry. But Carol declared she could not eat alone, and at that Erica gave in.

'I ought to come and help you,' she said languidly.

'Nonsense. You stay where you are,' Carol told her. 'I shan't be long.'

So Erica lay there very quietly and stared into the fire. And when Carol came back with the supper tray, she looked up almost tranquilly.

'All right?' Carol smiled.

Erica didn't answer. She scarcely seemed to hear.

'I've been thinking, Carol,' she said slowly. 'And I realise now that there's only one thing I can do.'

Carol looked anxious. She put down the tray on the table and came across the room.

'And what's that, Erica?'

'I shall just have to leave him,' said Erica calmly.

Carol didn't answer at once. She stood there biting her lips and looking very thoughtful.

'You're sure that's what you really want to do?' she said, speaking very gently. 'It isn't just a sort of desperate impulse that you'll regret afterwards.'

'I shall regret it—yes, of course,' Erica said slowly. 'One always regrets a decision like that at some time, I suppose. But there isn't really anything else to do. It would be—oh, untrue to myself and to my love if I stayed now. He's said so plainly that he doesn't want me, and if now, in spite of everything, he's going to stay at Dreda's beck and call, it's all wrong that I should submit meekly and accept that as the natural thing.'

'Well, I'm glad you're showing a little natural anger at last,' declared Carol.

Erica shook her head with a faint smile.

'It's not anger, exactly, Carol. That's all over now. It's just that, quite suddenly, I know it's the right thing to do. In a way, I forced myself into his life——'

'Nonsense,' interrupted Carol energetically. 'He *asked* you to marry him, didn't he?'

'Yes, I know. But it was I who understood the—false values of the arrangement. Not he. Looking back, I think perhaps I ought to have been frank with him then.' She broke off with a sigh. 'I don't know. It's so difficult to tell now. But, anyway, as things are, it's just the fact of my

101

being there which is forcing him into doing horrid, unhappy things which aren't really natural to him.'

'Well, darling, I'm not really following the logic of this,' Carol told her. 'And I have an idea you're muddling things a little, but if you think it's best to leave him, I'm all for seconding the motion. My reasons are probably a bit different from yours, but, at any rate, we've arrived at the same conclusion. Now just eat your supper before it spoils, and let's discuss what you mean to do.'

Only Carol, thought Erica, could contrive to talk as though leaving your husband were as unimportant as arranging a shopping expedition. But it was that blessedly matter-of-fact air of hers which actually made her so comforting. You couldn't be hysterical when she was urging you to try a new brand of cream cheese.

'I shall go this week-end,' Erica said slowly, as though working out her thoughts aloud. 'While he's away in London.'

Carol paused in the act of buttering a piece of bread.

'Do you mean without saying anything? Won't you have things out with him first?'

'No!' Erica spoke almost violently. 'I've done all the "having things out" that I can possibly stand. Another scene would just drive me crazy.'

'Yes, no doubt you're quite right.' Carol's voice was soothing again. And after a moment's pause she added: 'What will you do? Leave the time-honoured letter of explanation?'

'I suppose so.' Erica frowned a little. 'I know it sounds silly and melodramatic, but I don't know quite what else one does in—in the circumstances.'

'One might just clear out and leave him guessing,' Carol suggested laconically.

But Erica shook her head at once.

'No, that would be hateful. It would mean such miserable questioning and uncertainty.'

'What—for him?'

'Well, yes.'

Carol thoughtfully took a bite out of her slice of bread and butter.

'You are a funny girl,' she said. 'When anyone's got as far as hating her husband enough to leave him, it seems weird to me to bother about his peace of mind.'

'But I don't hate him, Carol. I don't!' Erica looked terribly distressed.

'All right.' Carol patted her arm. 'Let's not bother about that. Have you any idea where you'll go?'

'Yes—London,' Erica said, after only a second's thought. 'It's fairly easy to get a job there, I imagine, and it's easy to lose yourself, and perhaps it's easy to—forget there, too.'

For a moment her mouth quivered, but she pressed her lips firmly together and steadied them again.

'I've got about a couple of hundred pounds in my account. I didn't spend nearly all my allowance. I can draw out almost all of that.' It helped, somehow, to be concentrating so determinedly on these practical details. 'I must stock up the deep freeze, it's been getting low, and things like that.' She was almost thinking aloud by now. 'And then—I'll leave by the Saturday night train.'

'That means arriving in London on Sunday morning,' Carol pointed out practically.

'Yes, I know. But I want to go just as soon—as Oliver has gone. He'll leave by the morning train on Saturday ,and I can't spend a night in that house alone. Not—not when we've been there together.' Erica's face went down on her hands.

'You could stay here, easily,' Carol told her earnestly.

'I know, Carol dear.' Erica looked up again with quick gratitude. 'But I'd rather get away at once. Really I would.'

'Very well.' Carol made no further objection. 'But you'll come here to me in the evening for a good meal first, won't you? *Promise* me.' She looked suddenly terribly serious.

'Yes, I promise.' Erica gave her a faint smile. 'I should want to come to you anyway, you know. I couldn't—go without seeing you at the last.'

Carol nodded briefly to hide the fact that she was very much touched.

'And if there's anything you want done——'

'Oh, there won't be,' Erica assured her. 'It all seems so terribly simple. That's why it's so—difficult to believe.'

Carol looked at her with affectionate sympathy.

'Well, just try to remember one thing, dear. One *does* get over absolutely anything. I know it's awfully easy to say that when it's someone else's trouble, but it is true.'

'Yes, I know,' whispered Erica. 'I'll try—to think—of that.'

But, long afterwards, when Carol had insisted on taking her home, and she was safely upstairs in bed in her own room again, Erica remembered that remark of Carol's. And she thought—'But the real truth is that I don't *want* to get over it. I'd rather have the thought of Oliver in my heart, however much it may hurt, than just feel blank about him.'

The next two days were very difficult. They could scarcely be anything else.

In an odd way, Oliver seemed to have taken to heart some of the things she had said, because he was very careful not to be overbearing and unreasonable to her. But the very fact that he was gentler and more—'human,' she supposed was the word—made the thought of leaving him all the harder.

On Saturday morning, Erica felt it was almost beyond her powers of endurance to go down and face him across the breakfast table, knowing all the time that this was their last meal together. She had thought in the last few weeks that she had hated these breakfasts. Now, she knew that even this silent companionship was better than the awful, inescapable fact that she just would not be there at all in future.

She handed him his coffee, and sat there stirring her own absently—round and round and round—until she realised what she was doing, and hastily stopped. She sipped the coffee nervously then, instead. But it made her feel dreadfully sick.

Oliver was very little more at ease than she was. She knew it from the rapid way he kept on turning the leaves of his newspaper, without apparently finding anything that could hold his attention.

And then, finally, he pushed back his chair and got up.

104

'I must go, I'm afraid,' he said, but still without looking at her.

'Yes—or else you'll miss your train.' Erica thought her voice didn't sound so much calm as just stupid.

'Erica——' He stopped, and then went on doggedly, 'I'm sorry you're making yourself so unhappy about this. But in the circumstances I'm not prepared to give up this visit to London, just because you——'

'I know,' she interrupted him, but quite quietly still. 'It's simply that we could never see each other's point of view about this. We'll just—leave it at that, shall we?'

He looked almost as though he were going to say something else, but instead he shrugged his shoulders with a brief, 'As you like,' and went over to put on his coat which had been brought down and was lying across a chair.

She watched him dumbly.

This was the end, she kept on telling herself, but the fact didn't reach her consciousness.

He was ready now. His overnight case, she supposed, was in the hall. There was nothing to do but to say good-bye.

He said it quite calmly, almost casually, just as if he were going off to a business meeting—'Good-bye, Erica.'

'Good-bye.' Her voice seemed to come from a long way off.

He couldn't know, of course, that this was the end, that they were saying good-bye for ever. To him it was just a brief interval of a couple of days.

She watched him until he reached the door, and then, involuntarily, she spoke his name—'Oliver'.

He turned at once. Perhaps it was something in her face which made him come back to where she was standing before he said:

'What is it?'

She didn't reply for a moment. And then:

'I know it must sound absurd to you, but—will you kiss me?'

He looked extremely startled, so much so that she thought he would refuse her. But, instead, he took her quite gently by her shoulders.

'Is that really what you want, Erica?'

She nodded. And he bent his head at once and kissed her mouth.

She didn't say anything. She just put her hands up round his face, perhaps to prolong the moment. She hadn't ever meant to do that again, of course, but for a second she forgot—and this time he did nothing violent about it. He drew down her hands almost at once, it was true, but gently.

'I wish you wouldn't. You make me feel an unconscionable brute,' he said rather shortly. Then, quite incredibly, he kissed first one palm and then the other before he let her hands go and, without another word, walked out of the room and out of the house.

Erica could never remember very clearly afterwards just how she spent the rest of that day. She did the shopping as planned, then wandered from room to room of the house as if saying good-bye, restless and unable to settle—then she packed what she thought would be most useful to her now that she was going to be a girl on her own once again, earning her living.

Her explanation to the housekeeper that she was going away for a short visit sounded rather feeble to her, but it was accepted without any apparent surprise.

Was she leaving an address for letters and so on to be forwarded to her?

No, she was not leaving an address.

Oh, well, perhaps she would not be away long enough to make it worth while having anything sent on?

She made the best answer she could to that, and then escaped upstairs again to her own room.

There was only one thing left to do, and that was the letter to Oliver. Much the most difficult task of all, of course. She sat for ages at her writing desk, staring at a blank sheet of paper, and when she finally managed to write something, it seemed to her inadequate and pointless:

'Dear Oliver, I know it must seem melodramatic and stupid for me to run away like this and leave you a note, like some character in fiction, but I simply haven't the courage to face any more discussions——'

It looked silly and spineless written down, but it was the literal truth, so it must just stand.

'There isn't really any point in our going on together like this. For me it's wretched and, somehow, degrading, and I don't think it can be much better for you. That sounds as though I am blaming you. I'm not, really, although I know I said some very harsh things on Wednesday evening. The fact is that the whole idea of our marriage was wrong from the beginning, and, that being so, there is nothing to do but say good-bye before we have even forgotten that we had some happy weeks together.

'I want to tell you that I'm terribly, bitterly sorry about Dreda's letter. I know I acted very badly over it, but I honestly thought that it would mean more misery than happiness to you if she came back into your life. Try to forgive me, and if you don't want to remember me as your wife, please remember me occasionally as the secretary whom you once made very happy by telling her that she was "above all—faithful."

'I won't send you my love, for I know you don't want it. But because you cannot resent this from anyone—God bless you.—ERICA.'

When it was finished, she sealed it hastily and just wrote 'Oliver' on the envelope. Then she took it to his room.

She felt a little queer, going in there, rather as though she were intruding. She had scarcely ever been in before. The one time they had been together in this house he had come to her room. But she must not think of that now. It was sad and pointless when everything was so completely over.

She looked round for somewhere to leave the note. The dressing-table was the most obvious place, she supposed. And then she stopped in some surprise, because on the dressing-table, in a tiny frame, was a snapshot he had taken of her on their honeymoon.

There didn't seem very much reason for his having it there now, but somehow it gave her a faint feeling of comfort to see that he had not removed it. She propped the note against the photograph and went out of the room.

It was not until afterwards that she thought there was something symbolical in the fact that the letter must blot out the photograph. But the time for fancies—melancholy or otherwise—was over now. She had to be sensible and practical.

She telephoned for the taxi herself, for, somehow, she didn't want any half curious maid standing about, wondering. And then she carried down her case, and went out of the house without a word of good-bye to anyone.

Erica was glad that the distance to Carol's flat was so short. There was not very much time to think. It was going to be awful saying good-bye to Carol—much worse than when she had left the flat to be married, because then they had known that they could still see each other more or less when they liked.

Besides, Carol had grown very much dearer during the unhappy weeks of her married life.

Still, it was all just part of the break. It had to be faced. She had been lucky to have Carol for so long. Now she would have to stand entirely on her own feet. Perhaps it would be good for her.

But was it ever good to be so lonely? Oh, if only she hadn't got to say good-bye to Carol, too. She'd said good-bye to Oliver and been quite brave about it. Now she must be brave about this too.

But if only she need not have had to say good-bye to Carol. It was like a refrain in her mind.

'I was stupid to arrange it like this,' Erica thought as she got out of the taxi. 'We ought not to have had any real good-bye. I should have gone straight to the station and just written afterwards. Only I said I would come, so I must.'

She went up the stairs and rang the bell which was set right in the middle of the bright green door. She had never grown used to ringing at what had once been her own front door, and now it made her feel more of a stranger than ever.

It was funny to think how everything would go on here just the same when she had gone. Carol would miss her, of course, and often say, 'It's not a bit the same without Erica running in and out.' But by and by it would seem natural not to have her, and Carol wouldn't even remark on it any more.

And then Carol opened the door.

She already had her cheeky little cap pulled over her bright hair, so evidently she was coming to the station. She just smiled and stood aside for Erica to come in.

In the hall there were a couple of suitcases and a tote bag.

'Whose are those?' Erica said stupidly, though she knew Carol's blue case perfectly well.

'Mine.'

'But—but why?' Erica's heart was suddenly beating wildly.

'I'm coming too, of course. You didn't think I'd let you go alone, did you?'

'Oh, Carol,' Erica said. And then again, because there didn't seem to be anything else to say, 'Oh, *Carol*!'

Carol laughed and put her arm round her.

'All right. I know all the arguments against it——'

'Your job,' interrupted Erica.

'I've thrown it up. I'm dead sick of it anyway. I want a change. *I* want to go to London too. They weren't very keen on my going off at such short notice, but I said I had to rush away and nurse a sick aunt. If they didn't believe it they had to pretend they did.'

'But it's absolutely crazy, dear.' Erica felt she ought to make these feeble protests, but really she wanted to sing aloud with happiness for the first time for weeks.

'Yes, of course,' Carol agreed equably. 'But what's the good of living at all if you don't do crazy things sometimes?'

'No one but you would do anything quite so mad,' Erica said, with a little shake of her head.

'No, I know. That's what makes me such an interesting character. Now come and have a meal before we go, and I'll tell you all about how I managed to sub-let the flat with the furniture and everything. I thought it best to let it all go like that, because goodness knows how long it will be before we have a place of our own again.'

Erica scarcely said anything. She let Carol run on, almost without comment, simply allowing the warm tide of relief to flood over her.

She wouldn't be alone. She wouldn't have to go away alone on that dreadful night train. Carol would be with her.

Carol was saying how well they would manage until they both found jobs again. They would live in a girls' club so as not to spend too much of their small capital. And then, later on, they would have a little flat together again. And Erica was not to suppose that life had stopped. It was going to begin all over again with all sorts of exciting possibilities.

Erica smiled.

'Carol dear, I can't say a quarter of the things I want to, but in future when people speak of angels, I shan't see bright cardboard creatures with white wings, I shall just see you.'

'Nonsense.' Carol hugged her. 'You mustn't get these inflated ideas of my good qualities, or there'll be a nasty shock for both of us when the truth comes out. And don't say any more or we shall both begin to cry, and then we shall miss the train.'

So Erica said no more, but she secretly wondered if anyone had ever had a better friend than she had in Carol.

Even Carol had very little to say as they hastily finished their meal. Then they called another taxi and took their way to the big, draughty, rather empty station, where the London train stood waiting, the last great heaps of mail-bags being tossed aboard.

It was a strange journey. Night journeys always were a little unreal, Erica supposed, but this one was exactly like a dream. It was not the time of year when many people chose to travel, so they had the compartment to themselves and were able to lie down.

Carol slept contentedly almost at once, but Erica only in snatches. And as soon as the first cold light of dawn began to streak the sky, she sat up and watched the flying landscape.

It was hard to realise, even now, what an immense step

she had taken—in some ways, even bigger than the one she had made when she married Oliver.

For months before she had married him, Oliver had been in her every thought, and so even her strange marriage had only been a logical extension of what had gone before. But now all that was ended. An entirely new set of values must take its place.

Ah, well, Carol had said that you did get over everything. Perhaps you did get used to everything in time, too.

It was still depressingly early when they reached London. But a hot breakfast and the discovery of quite a pleasant club, where they could live very reasonably, served to raise their spirits.

Carol decreed that they should not even think about work and responsibilities for the day, and Erica found that she was more than willing to fall in with the suggestion that they should laze.

That part of her mind which was concerned with Oliver seemed curiously numb, as though she had had a partial anaesthetic. No doubt she would wake to a sharper realisation of things later on, but as it was, she just felt curiously and slackly contented to be with Carol and not face any problem for the moment.

'It's just as Carol said,' Erica reflected. 'It *is* a new life beginning, and I must try not to carry over any regrets from the old one. Oh, Oliver, my dear, I'm sorry, I'm sorry it should all have ended like this. But there's just not a single link left. And that is how it must be.'

That thought was still uppermost in her mind when she started next day on her search for a job.

A friendly girl at the club advised both her and Carol that answering advertisements was rather apt to waste postage and shoe-leather.

'You try Miss Dudenell's Agency. She's very so-so and a bit prim and proper, but she gets hold of some good jobs.'

So they presented themselves before the unimpeachable Miss Dudenell. And, with the thought of that very final break still in her mind, Erica described herself as a widow, with scarcely a moment's hesitation.

Miss Dudenell noted down full particulars about them, and immediately sent Carol off to a secretarial post in a dress house. Then she turned to Erica. 'Here is something that might suit you. A Dr. Sallent—here's the address—wants a clerk-receptionist who can also keep his books. You might try that.'

It was not very easy to find Dr. Sallent's house. Erica was misdirected twice, and by the time she did reach it she could scarcely put one foot in front of the other.

'It's ridiculous to feel like this,' Erica told herself. 'But I suddenly feel so dreadfully tired.'

A very neat-looking maid opened the door, and asked if she would mind waiting while the doctor 'finished his surgery.'

Erica said she didn't mind, but in reality she just didn't care. Her head ached dreadfully. It felt very, very heavy, and the rest of her curiously light, as though she were scarcely really there.

'I wish he'd come. Oh, I wish this were over,' Erica thought.

And then when he did come—a tall, dark, pleasant man in the middle forties—she found it quite difficult to struggle to her feet and stand there while he shook hands with her.

Fortunately he made her sit down again at once, and she tried to keep her mind on the problem of answering his enquiries.

She had been rather cold when she first came in. Now she felt almost feverishly hot, and for the first time she thought wildly, 'Surely I'm not going to be ill. That would be too awful!'

She missed what Dr. Sallent was saying and had to ask him to repeat it. That frightened her terribly. She must not do this. He would think her a hopeless wool-gatherer. He would——

Her thoughts slipped again, and then she heard him say from a long way off, 'Are you ill, Mrs. Leyne?'

And the next thing she knew was that she was trying not to swallow some queer-tasting stuff that he was telling her to drink.

112

After a moment she obeyed him, and then the outlines of the room began to clear again.

'I'm so sorry—I'm so sorry,' Erica stammered. 'I never do—that sort of thing—in the usual way.'

'That's quite all right. I began to wonder if you really had come as a prospective secretary or as a patient.' The doctor smiled kindly. 'But really you mustn't worry about it.'

He looked at her, however, with a little concern, and by and by he began to ask her one or two questions about herself. Nothing to do with her secretarial qualifications—strictly about how she felt in herself.

Erica didn't really much want to answer, but it was not easy to avoid it, and she soon found she had owned to feeling a good deal more unwell than she had let herself think lately.

After a while, he glanced at the introduction card from Miss Dudenell.

'You are a widow, I understand, Mrs. Leyne?' he said in that very sympathetic voice which inspired confidence.

It was much more difficult to tell the absurd little lie to him than it had been to Miss Dudenell, but finally she got out, 'Yes.'

'But you lost your husband very recently?'

'Well——' Erica paused. It was no good. She really couldn't keep up this subterfuge. Lying came so badly to her.

She stared helplessly at the doctor, and after a moment he smiled and said:

'It isn't any business of mine, of course, but I suppose this statement about your being a widow isn't quite accurate?'

'No,' Erica admitted almost in a whisper. 'But do you mind? I mean, from the point of view of choosing a secretary.'

'Oh'—he seemed to have forgotten the problem of the secretary for the moment—'I wasn't thinking of it from my point of view just then. Merely from yours.'

It was rather nice of him to put it that way, she thought, and presently she said:

'We—we just separated.'

'I see.' He looked thoughtful. And then, 'Don't think me very interfering, Mrs. Leyne, but isn't it perhaps possible that you might—well, come together again?'

'Oh, no,' Erica said quickly, thinking of how deliberately every link had been broken. A new life—that was what it was to be. A new life with nothing to link it with the old one. 'There's no question of it at all,' she added a little breathlessly.

'Well.' The doctor smiled very slightly. 'I wish you would reconsider that in the light of what I suppose is a new factor to you. You see, you're going to have a baby, Mrs. Leyne, and I feel this isn't quite the moment for you to be separating from your husband.'

CHAPTER V

'GOING to have a baby? *I* am?' Erica smiled slowly. 'Why, how wonderful!' And then, as practical considerations rose in her mind—'At least, it's very awkward too, of course.'

'It quite often is.' The doctor watched her a little amusedly. 'These things are really much better shared with one's husband, you know.'

'Oh, no.' Erica spoke quickly, and an expression of dismay clouded her face. She was thinking suddenly how horrified Oliver would have been to know that there was this amazing bond between them. Why, he had not even wanted *her* there, just loving him and trying not to be a nuisance. He certainly would not want her child—'our child' —thought Erica, and smiled again in spite of everything.

'Well, Mrs. Leyne, of course you know your own business best'—Dr. Sallent sounded a little as though he thought she did not, but was too polite to say so. 'I won't try to urge any advice upon you, one way or the other. But is there any way in which I can be of assistance to you?'

'You mean, of course, that I can't possibly have the job now?' Erica suddenly faced that ugly aspect of the situation, and it made her pale a little.

The doctor, however, was comforting.

'There really isn't any reason why you shouldn't take on a job for some months yet,' he told her, 'provided it's not too strenuous. But I'm afraid that as far as this job is concerned, it wouldn't do. You see, I should like to keep an eye on you as a patient, if I may, and a doctor has to have a quite exaggerated regard for appearances'—he paused and smiled regretfully—'especially if he is unmarried.'

'Yes, of course, I see.' Erica smiled slightly too, and hoped that her anxiety was not too obvious.

But Dr. Sallent had evidently decided to take the question of her welfare very thoroughly into his capable hands.

'Now the problem is, naturally, to find you another job in

place of the one I've just had to refuse you. I take it that the matter is—well, a bit pressing?'

'It's terribly kind of you to bother,' Erica said earnestly, 'but, yes, it *is* very important, I'm afraid.'

'It shouldn't be too difficult.' The doctor smiled as though finding jobs for stray patients was all in a day's work. And after a moment's thought he added, 'I have a friend who is the matron of a big children's clinic. She employs quite a large clerical staff, because she does a lot of work, too, in connection with the children's pages of various papers. I don't see why there shouldn't be an opening for you there.'

Erica's eyes brightened, and Dr. Sallent smiled.

'You would like that?'

'Oh, I'd love it,' Erica said fervently.

'Well, it would be a nice atmosphere for you, and you'd probably pick up some hints that would come in useful later.' The doctor laughed a little. 'I mustn't promise that there will be a vacancy, of course, but I know it is work that is always extending.'

'I can't possibly tell you how grateful I am.' Erica's mouth trembled slightly as she thought how completely the world seemed to have changed since she had stumbled in here so weary and hopeless.

If she got this job, and could manage carefully on her salary, she could use her capital for all the expenses of having the baby, and then——

It *was* a new life. An indescribably beautiful and exciting new life. But strange, strange, strange—it was indissolubly linked with the old life, after all.

Dr. Sallent came with her to the door and shook hands very kindly.

'I'll let you know to-morrow about this job,' he told her. 'Go home now and have a good night's rest, and don't worry about things. They'll work out splendidly, you'll see.'

'Thank you,' Erica said in a very low voice. And she thought what a lot of kind people there were in the world after all.

In the bus, on the way back to the club, she sat staring out at the lighted streets. She didn't feel weary and

116

dispirited and hopeless any more. She felt eager and excited.

She knew now, of course, why she had tired so easily and seemed to have lost all her usual initiative. But, once she had readjusted things so that she would not tire herself physically, she felt that her old zest for life would be as keen as ever.

'Poor darling Carol!' Erica thought with affectionate remorse. 'I have been flopping on her lately. But now I'll be quite different. Oh, I wonder what she'll say!'

Carol was sitting on the side of her bed, mending a slip when Erica came in.

'You're only just in time for supper, pet,' she told her. 'In fact, there's the bell. We'll tell each other the news afterwards.'

'It's nearly all nice news, Carol,' Erica smiled.

'Is it? That's grand,' said Carol. 'I landed my job too,' she added casually.

'Did you? So we're both fixed up all right.'

'Yes.' Carol glanced at her. 'And I wish I could tell you how good it is to see you all happy and excited again.'

'Oh'—Erica looked rather surprised. And then she thought—well, that was just how she did feel: all happy and excited.

And the feeling persisted all through the good, nourishing but decidedly uninteresting meal.

When they had come upstairs again, Carol's first remark was:

'Funny how you miss your own place, once you've had one. I don't think club life will suit me very long. It's all right when you've never done anything else, but I vote the first thing we aim at is our own place again. We'll look round and see what we can find. I only let the other flat and our furniture for three months, so we could have our own things sent down here.'

'Yes.' Erica gave a rather slow smile of pleasure, like a child who had been offered a treat. 'It'll be wonderful to have our own place again. In fact, we should have to.'

'Oh, should we?' Carol looked amused. 'Now tell me why you've been beaming quietly all supper time.'

'I'm going to have a baby.'

'You're *what*?'

'Going to have a baby.'

'My dear girl, that's rather serious, isn't it? Don't say it as though you've stumbled on a diamond mine.'

'I think a baby's much nicer than a diamond mine,' Erica said tranquilly.

'Do you? A diamond mine is much more unusual. Personally, I'm all for that,' Carol retorted grimly.

Erica laughed.

'Won't you like *my* baby, Carol?'

'Yes, of course. I shall probably develop into one of those revolting adopted aunts who address defenceless infants as "Diddums." But do you mind descending to the rather more practical considerations? When, where and how do you propose to have and support this child?'

'Oh, I'll tell you all about it,' Erica exclaimed.

'I wish you would. And put your feet up on this chair or something. I have an idea that's the correct thing to do if you're seriously going to have a baby.'

Erica laughed again—a little surprised to find that she laughed so easily now—did exactly as she was told, and then proceeded to give Carol an account of her visit to Dr. Sallent, finishing up with a description of the probable job at the children's clinic.

'Hm. And you're just as pleased as punch about the whole thing, I take it?' Carol remarked at the end.

'I'm happy again, Carol,' said Erica with great simplicity. And at that Carol's face softened.

'Then I'm delighted too, my dear. It's certainly a weird complication in the life of two business girls. But I don't see why we shouldn't manage all right. Certainly we shall have to find our own place now. I think this club is only for spinsters or those who have been decently widowed, so this exploit of yours might have an awkward interpretation put on it.'

'You are ridiculous,' Erica told her contentedly. 'But I think everything is going to be heavenly—oh, Carol, tell me now about you,' she exclaimed, remembering suddenly that there was Carol's news too. 'How did you get on?'

'Well, of course, I can't hope to rival you in sensation,' Carol told her. 'I'm afraid any small announcement of mine pales before the magnitude of your effort.'

'Come on. Stop being silly and tell me all about it,' Erica said, thinking how pleasantly like the old days it was to be chaffing with Carol again.

So Carol, in her turn, gave a spirited description of the dress house where she was to start her career as secretary-cashier the next day.

'She isn't really a bit put out about the baby,' thought Erica amusedly. 'She takes everything in her stride. She'll make a success of this job of hers too.'

And afterwards, when they were in bed and the light was out, Erica said, 'I think you'll make a splendid cashier, Carol. Businesslike and pleasant, but very firm.'

'Thanks, darling,' Carol said rather sleepily. 'And I think you'll make a splendid mother. Not quite firm enough, but awfully sweet. And anyway, I'll be there to supply the discipline.'

Erica laughed softly, and lay there for quite a long time before she went to sleep, thinking, 'Yes. I'll be a splendid mother. I will, I *will*!'

During the next week or two, Erica thought more than once how extraordinary it was that, after an unbearably difficult part of your life, you would suddenly come upon a smooth, easy stretch that was just like a wide pleasant meadow on a sunny day.

A very great deal of the pleasantness, she knew, was due to Dr. Sallent and his unfailingly kind interest in her welfare.

'It sounds to me as though the man has fallen for you,' declared Carol, when she heard of his care and trouble to see that the job at the clinic really came Erica's way. But Erica smiled and said, no, that was nonsense.

And as soon as she saw him with his friend, the matron of the clinic, Erica knew that any 'falling' on his part had been done long ago.

'Well, I can quite understand any man being in love with her,' thought Erica earnestly as she looked into Mrs. Tait's smiling blue eyes, and warmed to her kindly, practical manner.

She was quite a youngish woman still—some years off forty, Erica guessed—but her smooth black hair already had a good deal of grey in it. And although her eyes smiled so easily, there was a suggestion of gravity in the set of her mouth that was curiously like resignation.

'I suppose she is a widow, and has been very unhappy,' reflected Erica. 'But perhaps, later on, she'll marry my nice Dr. Sallent and be happy again. I'd like that to happen.'

She was surprised and a little amused to find how personally interested she felt in them. But, even from the first, the interest seemed mutual, for Mrs. Tait took Erica very much to her heart.

'I think it's a lovely idea to have someone on the staff who obligingly supplies us with a baby of our own,' she declared with a laugh. 'He or she will have to be the practical proof of the perfection of our methods.'

'It's awfully nice of you to look at it like that,' Erica said. 'And I *will* manage to be really useful to you, too.'

'I'm certain you will,' Mrs. Tait assured her kindly.

Erica had a shrewd suspicion that even if she had proved hopeless at the work, Mrs. Tait would have found it hard to bring herself to the point of sending her away. But, as it was, she was delighted with Erica's practised and efficient ways of working.

'My dear girl, you really have a wonderful idea of method,' she said once, when Erica had been with her a few weeks. 'Wherever did you get your training?'

Erica very nearly said, 'From my husband,' but just bit the words back in time. Instead, she said slowly:

'Well, the man I used to work for was a little—exacting.'

'I think he must have been,' Mrs. Tait answered with a smile, but she failed to notice how silent Erica had become.

Even to speak of Oliver like that, without so much as the mention of his name, brought him back suddenly as though he stood before her—big, dark, difficult and indescribably dear.

How extraordinary of her ever to have imagined that she could escape from the thought of him, that she could break off all connection with the life she had shared with him. She—who was going to have his child.

Suddenly she wanted him—terribly, overwhelmingly, in a way that almost brought tears to her eyes. Oh, what would it have been like if things had been different, if they had been sharing the thought of their baby together?

She liked her work immensely. It was not very exacting and it was exciting to feel all the while that she was learning all about the job of being a good mother.

Most of the time she felt very well, and they took good care of her at the clinic, just as Carol insisted on taking good care of her at home.

With all her apparently careless and slapdash ways, Carol was really a good and sympathetic manager, and she was as eager as Erica herself that everything should be done properly.

After a while they did find a little flat, not far from the clinic, which looked like suiting them very well, and it was Carol who said that she would go back to their old home and arrange about having the furniture moved.

Something about that unsettled Erica badly, and made her terribly restless and unhappy again. She said nothing about it to Carol, but she could scarcely bear the thought that, while Carol would go back to the very town where Oliver was—might even, by some queer chance, see him— to her the place was closed.

'You don't really mind being left, do you?' Carol said anxiously. 'It's only a couple of days, you know. I shall be back by the Saturday evening.'

'I know, dear, I know. It's all right. I don't mind a bit,' Erica protested. But she had a wild impulse to say, 'I'm coming too. I *must* come too.'

And when Carol had gone, she had her first real fit of weeping since she had been told she was to have the baby.

Afterwards, she pulled herself together, scolded herself thoroughly, and vowed she would never do anything so stupid again. But it was a very serious Erica who went to the clinic that day.

Mrs. Tait noticed it at once but, having once been assured that Erica was feeling all right, she asked no more

121

questions. Only at the end of the day she said:

'Would you like to come home to dinner with me this evening? You're all on your own, aren't you?'

Erica accepted eagerly, and went home with Mrs. Tait in the little blue Mini which she drove herself.

The house was a charming place in Chelsea, near the river. It had a quaint, uneven appearance outside and unexpectedly spacious rooms inside. Evidently Mrs. Tait had a very good knowledge of antiques, for the place was a treasury of old furniture and china. Or perhaps, thought Erica, it was the husband who had chosen so well.

She wondered a little about him, for there was no sign of him anywhere, not even a photograph. Perhaps Mrs. Tait was the kind of person who just couldn't bear any reminder of her dead husband near her. It looked like that, because the only photograph in the place was an excellent one of Dr. Sallent, which stood on the eighteenth-century harpsichord in the drawing-room and somehow dominated the room.

It was the first thing Erica noticed when they came in there after dinner.

'Oh, how good of Dr. Sallent,' she exclaimed, almost without thinking.

Mrs. Tait smiled.

'Yes. It's about the only one he ever had taken. Poor Jeremy, he hates being photographed as much as most men, but he had that one done to please me.'

'I think he would do most things to please you.' Erica said diffidently.

'Oh—yes, I suppose so,' Mrs. Tait agreed rather noncommittally.

'He's very fond of you, isn't he?' Erica felt it was the moment to put in a word for her nice Dr. Sallent.

'Yes, very.' Evidently from her voice the comment gave her pleasure but no surprise.

'I often think——' Erica stopped. Perhaps she was going a little too far.

'Yes? What do you think?'

The tone of that didn't suggest that Erica was being at all impertinent.

122

'Well, that you and Dr. Sallent will marry one day and be most awfully happy together.'

'We can't you know. My husband is still alive,' Mrs. Tait said with perfect calmness.

Erica was very much taken aback.

'Is he? I—I'm terribly sorry to have said anything like that. I just didn't think. I've always supposed—I don't know why—that your husband was dead.'

But Mrs. Tait didn't seem to mind at all what Erica had said.

'Yes, I know. It's very natural that you should think that, and it would be so much better if he were. He has been in a mental hospital for ten years now.'

She spoke so unemotionally that Erica scarcely took in the meaning of her words for a moment. Then, when she did, she put out her hand quickly.

'My dear, I'm dreadfully sorry. How very brave and calm you are about it,' she said gently.

Mrs. Tait smiled and patted her hand.

'Oh, yes, I'm quite calm nowadays. It isn't much good being anything else about the inevitable. And I would never feel easy in my mind if I—got rid of him.'

She spoke in short, almost impersonal sentences that were somehow much more telling than floods of eloquence. And after a moment she added:

'The worst part was when I met Jeremy, and we found out how we felt about each other.'

Erica was dumb with sympathy. Then she found her voice at last, to say a little defiantly:

'I think in a case like that, and when you absolutely can't marry, it's almost justifiable to—do the other thing.'

'Yes,' Mrs. Tait said slowly. 'Yes, I agree with you. But you can't if you're a doctor, you know. Not unless you're prepared to finish your career then and there. That's why I took my training and started the clinic. It gives us a chance of working together in a common interest.'

Erica was quite silent again. She was staggered at the way these two had met their terrible problem and worked it out to some bearable conclusion. When you were unhappy yourself and life seemed almost made up of your own problems, it was easy to forget that other people were facing difficulties too, that other tragedies were happening and other victories against circumstances being won.

'I won't forget again,' Erica told herself. 'I won't fret about Oliver any more. I'll think only of the fact that the baby is going to be mine and that I'm very, very lucky.'

But it was not quite as easy as that, of course. And, in fact, the very next evening, when Carol came home, Erica was consumed with eager impatience to know whether she had any news.

Although of what the 'news' could consist she herself hardly knew.

Carol, however, was perfectly willing to give an amusing and detailed description of the move, of her journey, of everything, in fact, so long as it entailed no mention of the one person of whom Erica wanted to hear.

At last, when Carol had apparently said all there was to say, Erica could keep silent no longer.

'Then you didn't—you didn't see Oliver, by any chance,' she said, avoiding Carol's eyes as though there were something a little guilty in her frantic desire to ask about him.

There was a moment's silence, and then Carol said:

'Do you really think it's any good talking about Oliver now, my dear? It only upsets you.'

Erica brushed that aside.

'You mean you *did* see him,' she exclaimed almost fiercely.

'Well, yes, I did.'

'Carol! Where? Did he speak to you? Oh, why didn't you tell me right away? I've been waiting—I've been waiting so long just to hear a word of him.'

Carol got up and came over to where Erica was sitting.

'I didn't tell you, because I hoped you wouldn't ask, and then we need not even mention him,' she said, putting her arm round Erica. 'I thought it was much the best thing. But since you *have* asked—yes, I did see him, just casually in the street, and—yes, he did speak to me.'

'What did he say?' It was not much more than a whisper.

'He asked if I knew where you were.'

'Oh, Carol!—and what did you tell him?'

'I told him I hadn't the least idea,' Carol said calmly.

'You told him—that? You lied to him?'

'Certainly I lied to him. It was the simplest way out, and I assure you that a lie to Oliver Leyne rests very lightly on my conscience.'

'But he must have known it wasn't the truth,' Erica said. Carol shrugged.

'I suppose so. In fact, he said as much.'

'Carol! Whatever did you say then?'

'Faced him out, of course, and said I was in a better position than he to say whether I were speaking the truth or not. Then I reminded him politely that he was no longer my boss, wished him good afternoon and left him.'

'How did he look, Carol? How did he look?'

'Much the same as usual. A bit glum,' Carol said in a matter-of-fact tone.

'You mean he looked unhappy?' Erica asked sharply.

'Well, he never looks joyous, does he?'

'*I've* seen him look joyous once or twice,' Erica said softly. 'Boyishly happy and gay. On our honeymoon.'

Carol said nothing, only watched Erica in silent pity.

Then Erica said:

'I think you should have said something, Carol—*something* that would have given him the chance——'

'My dear,' Carol interrupted firmly, 'if you want to re-establish a connection with Oliver, you can do so yourself any day that you like, by the simple expedient of ringing him up. If you don't, isn't it best to make the break complete, rather than flirt with these "ifs" and "ans"?'

It was Erica's turn for silence.

Then after a long while she put her head against Carol, a little as though it ached.

'You're right, of course. You're quite right,' she said with a sigh. 'I'll try not to talk like that again.'

And Erica was as good as her word. As the months slipped away she never mentioned Oliver again. They talked of the baby, of themselves, of Dr. Sallent, of Mrs. Tait, but never of Oliver. And Carol dared to hope that he was at last taking less of a place in Erica's thoughts.

Even when it came at last to the day that Erica was taken

away to the bright, pleasant little maternity home run in connection with the clinic, she still said nothing to Carol about Oliver. She just hugged her very tightly and said:

'Don't worry, I'll be all right. Come and see both of us as soon as they'll let you.'

Only much later, when the borderline between reality and thought had become lost in the crisis through which she was passing, did Erica break the silence of months. And there was one person—and one person alone—for whom she asked.

But by then, of course, she only had near her the people who had no idea that Oliver was almost a forbidden name, so she could say it as often as she liked.

'That's the husband, of course,' thought Dr. Sallent. 'Poor little girl, I wish she could have him. But perhaps he's just no good. Let's hope the baby will mean more happiness to her than he has.'

The last gleams of a very warm September sun were just filtering into the room when Erica came drifting back from what seemed a long, long journey. The strange, pungent smell of anaesthetics still hung about, making her feel dazed and vague, and she had the odd impression that she had been in some battle which had almost been too much for her.

Well, that was more or less the case, she supposed, with a confused recollection of what had gone before.

'What's that funny noise?' she heard herself say in a voice that didn't sound at all like her own.

Then someone laughed, and Erica realised that it was the nurse.

'That funny noise, Mrs. Leyne, is your son and heir making himself heard,' the nurse explained.

Erica thought she cried out, 'Bring him to me! Please bring him to me!' But it was really only a whisper.

And then something small and warm and very vocal was put down beside her.

She stared and stared at him. At the little pink face and the dozens of tiny chestnut curls which were like absurd replicas of her own. And as she did so, something seemed to

126

come alive right deep down inside her heart.

He was here—the baby she had been waiting for. *Her* baby. He was even idiotically like her. At least, his hair was.

With a delightful little laugh she feebly gathered him against her.

'Oh, darling, stop that awful noise, and unscrew your face and let me look at you,' she begged.

And, miraculously, the baby stopped crying at that moment. His short, thick lashes fluttered on his cheeks, and then flicked suddenly upwards—to show eyes that were not grey like her own at all, but wide and dark and beautiful, like Oliver's.

'Oh,' Erica said, and it was just a long sigh, but whether of joy or pain she scarcely knew, because they were so close together.

But after a while she supposed it must be joy, because nothing in the world seemed to matter any more except that her baby son was looking at her with Oliver's eyes.

CHAPTER VI

'IT's quite natural that *we* should think him the most wonderful baby in the world, Carol. But don't you think it's very funny and nice that everyone else here should think so too?' Erica said, when Carol had come in one evening on her usual visit.

'Nice but not at all funny,' amended Carol. 'He *is* the most wonderful baby in the world, so why shouldn't they have the intelligence to see it?'

Erica laughed, and looked very well satisfied with this logic.

'How are things going with you?' She looked at Carol affectionately over the top of the baby's head.

'So-so,' said Carol, who always said that, because she was too much of a fighter to admit it when things were bad, and too much of a good-natured cynic to admit that they could be good. 'I miss you at home, of course. It will be good to have you both back.'

'Yes, we'll be glad to be back, too,' Erica agreed.

'What are you going to call the infant?' Carol went on. 'Isn't it time we decided on a name for him?'

Erica looked surprised.

'I *have* decided long ago. He'll be Oliver, of course.'

Carol jerked up her eyebrows.

'He's rather a scrap for a name of three syllables, isn't he?' was all she said.

'I suppose we shall have a pet name for him, too,' Erica replied a little defensively.

'Most decidedly,' declared Carol, and Erica rather thought she meant, '*I* shan't call him Oliver.'

'The nurses all call him Bunny,' Erica offered in a placatory tone. 'I don't quite know why, but it seems to suit him.'

'Yes, it's silly but nice,' Carol conceded.

And, in the end, Bunny he became. Though once or twice Erica wondered with a little shocked amusement

128

whether the youngest representative of the house of Leyne ought to be known by anything quite so undignified. Old Mr. Leyne would have thought it idiotic, she supposed. But then perhaps if old Mr. Leyne had been the kind to call *his* son something 'silly but nice' when he was little, Oliver would never have been quite the difficult person he was, and—oh, all sorts of things might have been different.

But it was no good thinking about that now, so Erica firmly turned her thoughts to other things.

And there was a good deal to occupy them.

By the time she and Bunny came home, quite a large hole had been eaten in her capital, and Erica was absolutely determined not to take more from Carol than she could possibly help.

The girls shared the expenses of the flat equally, and, in a hundred little ways, Carol contrived to do and give extra things for Bunny, but Erica would not hear of her drawing on her own reserves to any real extent. That meant, of course, that the sooner she herself went back to work, the better. And a dozen times a day she felt grateful to Dr. Sallent for having seen to it that her work was actually at a children's clinic.

It was really surprisingly simple. Bunny merely came with her.

Fortunately, he was angelically good—'almost as good as we think he is,' Carol said. And all day he lived and slept in ideal conditions, while Erica did her work. He came in for rather more than his share of adulation from an adoring staff, but Erica managed to ward off some of the spoiling. Enough, she hoped, to keep his disposition from being ruined. Or so she told Carol.

'Nothing would ruin his disposition,' was all Carol said. 'He's like you—much too sweet and easily put upon. I hope they teach him to be a selfish little pig. They're the people who get on.'

Erica laughed protestingly.

'You'll have to give up saying those things when he's old enough to understand,' she warned Carol. 'Or he'll take them at their face value.'

'He understands now,' Carol declared. 'Look at the way

he watches me and stores up worldly wisdom.'

And certainly Bunny did watch her with his big dark eyes, and smiled almost every time she said anything specially ridiculous to him.

At first Erica had thought of him entirely as hers. Her responsibility and her happiness. But she wondered uneasily now whether it had been entirely right to assume that Oliver would have no interest in his son.

When Bunny was a month or two old, Dr. Sallent, too, said something which stirred up her doubts again. He had called in at the clinic on business, and took the opportunity to come and inspect Bunny, who was lying asleep in the large garden shelter attached to the clinic.

'Hm. There's no need to ask if he is all right.' Dr. Sallent smiled down at him.

'He's very well.' Erica smiled too. 'He never seems to be anything else.'

'No, he's a fine child. No wonder you're so proud of him.'

'Oh, dear, am I more disgustingly proud than most mothers?' Erica asked ruefully.

'No, no.' Dr. Sallent laughed as they turned to go into the house again. 'You have every justification, Mrs. Leyne. And you take your responsibilities well.'

Erica bit her lip slightly.

'Sometimes I wonder——' she began, and then stopped.

'Yes, I know. So do I,' Dr. Sallent said.

'Why, what do you mean? Did you know what I was going to say?'

'I think so. You wonder a little whether you ought to shoulder those responsibilities entirely alone,' the doctor suggested.

Erica nodded. Then she looked distressed.

'It isn't that I mind the responsibility at all,' she explained quickly. 'It's that I think perhaps it's a bit unfair to—to my husband.'

'Yes. And possibly to the little boy as well?'

'I hadn't thought of that,' Erica said in a troubled voice.

'Well, perhaps I'm wrong, of course. I don't pretend to

know the circumstances. But I've always had the impression that your husband is at any rate a fairly rich man.'

'Oh, yes. Very rich, as a matter of fact.' Erica so seldom thought about it that it came as something of a surprise now.

Dr. Sallent nodded.

'Money isn't necessarily of paramount importance,' he said carefully, 'but it can be a very big factor when it comes to bringing up a boy and educating him.'

'You mean, of course, that my husband could do much more for the child than I ever could?' Erica exclaimed sharply.

'Oh, no, I'm not saying that,' Dr. Sallent reassured her quickly. 'I don't know your husband, so I couldn't possibly venture an opinion on that. But what I do think is that, with so many material advantages for your little boy in the balance, it might perhaps be better to see if quarrels couldn't be made up and breakages mended.'

Erica looked startled.

'I don't know why,' she said slowly, 'but you always speak as though it can't be very much that keeps my husband and me apart, as though something might suddenly make it all fall into place one day. Why do you think that?'

The doctor smiled.

'Because, my dear child, it's perfectly obvious even to a middle-aged bachelor like myself that you're still very much in love with your husband. And that, after all, is half the problem solved.'

'Oh——' Erica looked a little nonplussed. Then she added sadly, 'But he doesn't love me, that's all.'

Dr. Sallent looked at her with lively pity, and privately thought the husband must be hard to please.

'Well, you know best, of course,' he said kindly. 'And there's no need to make any decisions about your baby yet. But just think it over again.'

Erica thought it over and over and over. And finally she said to Carol:

'Dr. Sallent rather thinks that I—that I should tell Oliver about Bunny.'

'Very likely. Men always hang together,' retorted Carol sharply. 'He doesn't know what he's talking about.'

'But there is something in it, Carol,' Erica sighed. 'Both from Oliver's point of view and Bunny's.'

Carol put down the work she was doing.

'There's nothing in it at all but a lot of false sentiment,' she said firmly. 'It's a bit late for Oliver to start being paternal now, and Bunny won't miss him if he never has him. I'm sorry to see all that money go,' she added with great candour, 'but I don't see how it can be helped.'

And after that Erica didn't say any more about telling Oliver.

It was about a couple of months later, when Bunny's first Christmas had come and gone, that Erica saw the announcement of a concert of chamber music by the Colin Lamb Quartet.

It was odd, seeing Colin's name like that in print, and suddenly it seemed to bring back Oliver's cynical yet kindly friend very clearly.

'Do you know,' she said on impulse to Carol, 'I'd simply love to go to this concert.'

'Well then, go, my dear. Why ever not?' Carol said. 'Bunny's quite old enough to be left now, and he'll be perfectly all right with me to look after him.'

'You're sure you don't mind?'

'Mind? No, of course not. I'm rather flattered at being left entirely in charge,' Carol assured her.

Erica smiled thoughtfully.

'I liked Colin Lamb,' she said slowly. 'He was genuinely kind at heart, for all his surface sophistication. And then he was fond of Oliver too and really understood him.'

Carol didn't answer the last part of that. She just said: 'I thought him a very good sort that one time I met him.'

'Oh, yes, of course, you met him at my wedding, didn't you?' It all seemed years ago. Erica had almost forgotten that lunch with the four of them together. It was like another life. Before—just an hour before—Dreda had come into her world and spoilt everything.

'Yes,' Carol said. 'After you two had gone off on—on your honeymoon, he took me to a matinée. We got quite

132

friendly, now I come to think of it. I'd forgotten all about it until now.'

Erica looked surprised.

'You never told me,' she said interestedly.

'No. There always seemed to be other things to talk about——' Carol stopped, because, of course, they both had to remember then what very unhappy things they had been. After a moment, she went on flippantly, 'I think he quite admired me by the end. At least, he told me I was the only deliberately shocking girl he'd ever met who really carried it off with charm and success.'

'Carol——' Erica laughed then. 'I think it's you and not I who ought to be going to this concert.'

But Carol shook her head emphatically.

'You can't really imagine me at a concert of chamber music, can you?' she said. 'Added to which, he probably wouldn't know me if he saw me now. And in any case'—she looked in some surprise at Erica—'you're not going round back-stage afterwards, are you? I mean, you don't intend to see him?'

'Oh, *no*!' Erica gave a half dismayed little laugh. 'It might lead to—oh, all sorts of complications. All I intend to do is to have a cheap ticket in the balcony, and hear him, just for the sake of—well, curiosity and friendship, I suppose.'

Carol nodded carelessly, perhaps a little relieved that Erica didn't even mention Oliver.

The night of the concert was cold and rather wet, and when Erica found that she had to stand in a queue to get her ticket she wondered just a little why she had been so anxious to come.

It was extraordinary to see Colin Lamb—actually someone she knew—come on to the platform and be received with applause. She didn't notice the other three much, until they all grouped themselves companionably in a little circle, as though they were going to enjoy the music as much as everyone else.

'It's just as though they were playing at a party,' thought Erica. And, once the music began, the impression deepened.

They seemed to be playing for their own sheer pleasure

133

in it, and anyone who cared to listen was very welcome to do so and share the pleasure with them.

So Erica listened. She listened so intently that she forgot everything else. And it was more than half way through the first item before her gaze wandered idly across the people in the stalls and came to rest on—Oliver.

Erica locked her hands together tightly and kept herself from trembling by an immense effort.

It was Oliver—her husband—Bunny's father. Neither of those descriptions seemed to make much impression as she repeated them to herself. It was just Oliver, the man she loved. And at that the tears came into her eyes.

She blinked them away because they made it so difficult to see him. As it was, he was such a long way off that she couldn't really tell how he was looking. Was it her imagination that the touch of grey in his hair had increased? Oh, if only she could see him better!

And then she noticed that the man next to her had a pair of opera glasses.

Wide-eyed with impatience, she waited until a pause in the music gave her a chance to speak.

'Please,' she whispered earnestly, '*Please* might I borrow your glasses just for a minute?'

'Certainly,' the young man said graciously. 'That fellow's left hand work is well worth watching.'

He didn't tell her which fellow—that would have been giving too much away—but in any case Erica was not interested in anybody's left-hand work.

Trembling, she turned the glasses on the audience.

How lucky that she had chosen a seat so much to the side. She would be able to see him quite well.

She couldn't tell whether it were tears or bad focusing that made the glasses so misty. Ah, that was better. It was much clearer now. It was wonderful! There was the woman in red who had been sitting quite near him, and the very bald man, and——

Oliver suddenly came into her field of vision, so clearly that he seemed to be beside her. It was as though he had been given back to her for a moment across time and space, and she gazed and gazed, her heart beating so high up in

134

her throat that it was difficult for her to breathe.

He was sitting with his head slightly bent, his face grave and attentive and just a little worn. And yes—there was quite a distinct touch of grey, just where his thick dark hair grew back from his temples. His left hand was holding an open programme on his knee, and, characteristically, his gloved hand was hidden under the programme.

Somehow, that last touch was so much more *her* Oliver than anything else about him. No one else in the hall knew why he did that. But she knew, and it made her heart ache, for him as well as for herself.

Reluctantly she lowered the glasses once more and gave them back to their owner. She had not looked at the platform once. Not one of the players interested her now. To tell the truth, she had forgotten there was a concert going on.

The interval came at last, and she saw Oliver get up to go out. He was so tall and commanding that he seemed to stand out even in a crowd like that. And when he finally disappeared through one of the doorways, Erica drew a long sigh and leaned back in her seat again as though some great tension had been relaxed.

Idly, she glanced at her programme to see what was in the second half. A laconic line of print stared back at her.

'Pianoforte—Dreda Canterley.'

Erica suddenly became quite still, unaware that people were filing back into the hall, that the interval was over and the concert about to resume.

All she knew was that Dreda was to play in the second half of the programme, and that was why Oliver was there.

It ought not really to have been such a shock to her. It was simply a logical extension of a situation she already knew existed. But somehow it came as a shattering blow.

She thought that if she could have got away now she would have. But here were the players again.

And, with them, Dreda.

Erica had known before all about how beautiful she was. But as she came in now, in a perfectly simple black dress, Erica thought, with a little catch at her heart, that any man would find her irresistible.

135

With terrible reluctance, Erica's eyes went to her husband. Curiously enough, however, Oliver was not even looking at Dreda. He seemed to be studying his programme. But that, perhaps, was only his way of hiding his feelings.

Erica didn't hear much of the rest of the programme. It was beautiful, of course. That much she knew. And she knew also that Dreda's playing was brilliant. But the evening was spoilt for her.

She watched Oliver again, but not with the same rather innocent pleasure. That, too, was spoilt, because she was trying frightenedly to read in his face what his feelings were. And she was quite unable to do so.

When it was all over Erica hardly knew whether she were glad or sorry. Until she saw that Oliver was going. Then she knew that the awful deprivation of having to lose even the sight of him was worse than anything else in life.

It was all over now. Oliver had gone. The hall was almost empty, and a few bored officials were going round picking up dropped programmes and saying, 'Hurry along, please,' mechanically to the stragglers.

Erica went out into the corridor, feeling like a child whose party was over and whose present turned out to be broken when she got it home.

Two girls, hurrying along, pushed past her, laughing and talking.

'Good, wasn't she?' said one. 'Even apart from the looks.'

'Yes,' agreed the other. 'Shall we go to the stage door?'

'Oh, I think so. That is, if it isn't raining still. I'd like to see what she's really like.'

Automatically Erica quickened her pace. She was not quite sure what she was going to do, but she didn't want to lose sight of those girls until she had decided.

Suppose *she* went to the stage door too. It might be quite easy to see without being seen, especially if there were a good many people.

Of course, Oliver might not come out that way, but since he knew two of the artists he would surely go round backstage.

She would have to be very careful not to be seen. She *would* be careful. And he wouldn't have the faintest idea that she was there, so it would be quite safe.

Erica had reached the stage door long before she had finished the argument with herself. There were not more than a handful of people there, but the light was poor, and she could stand half hidden, in any case, behind a jutting out piece of the wall.

The rain had stopped, but there was a cold little wind blowing, and more than once Erica shivered violently. It was silly to wait like this. She would only catch cold. She ought to be hurrying home to Bunny.

The thought of Bunny warmed her a little. But even he seemed somehow remote compared with the idea that Oliver might come out of that doorway at any moment.

And then there was a slight stir of excitement, the swing doors opened and out came Dreda, with a white fur cape over her black dress.

She was laughing a little—evidently bright and happy —and she paused for a moment to give an autograph to a very young admirer. Everyone was looking at her and smiling too, because she was really so good to look at.

Everyone, that was, except Erica. She was watching the man who had come out with Dreda, who opened the door of her car for her, who got in after her, and finally drove away with her.

The man was Oliver.

Even when the car had gone, Erica went on standing there, although the rain had begun again and was falling on her face and neck in the little cold drops. Nearly everyone else had gone, because it had been Dreda they had all wanted to see.

Erica, too, had seen the one person she had come to see, but she just went on standing there, staring at the place where the car had been.

She'd been a fool to come, of course. What else had she expected to see? Wasn't it perfectly natural that he should come out with Dreda? take her out to supper? escort her home?

Yes. It was perfectly natural. Carol would have said it

was all she could expect, and that it only showed how use-less it was ever to think about him in this sentimental way again.

Very slowly, Erica turned away at last, without very much idea of where she was going.

And as she did so, someone came up quickly behind her and put a hand on her shoulder.

'Why, Mrs. Leyne—Erica! What are you doing here? No, please don't run away. I want to speak to you.'

And with something rather like panic Erica turned quickly again—to find Colin Lamb looking down at her with kindly astonishment.

'Oh,' Erica said rather helplessly. 'Oh, I—I've just been to your concert, you know.'

That was rather stupidly obvious, of course, but he didn't seem to think it silly.

'Have you? I wish I'd known before. I'd have looked out for you.'

Not a word about Dreda. Not a word about Oliver. But then perhaps he scarcely would rush into talking about them, considering the circumstances.

The one or two people still round the stage door glanced at them curiously.

'Look here, do let me take you somewhere for supper,' exclaimed Colin. 'I'm starving after all that work, and I hate eating alone.'

'I'm sorry, I can't. I've got to go home to my baby,' Erica blurted out.

'To your—what? Oh, my dear——' He suddenly looked very kindly. 'Well, then let's go by taxi. No, really, I in-sist.'

And before Erica could protest any more she found her-self handed into a taxi, where the friendly gloom was rather comforting, considering that she might want to hide a good deal.

'Now'—she saw from the passing lamp-light that he had turned interestedly towards her—'do tell me about it. I didn't know you had a baby.'

'No, nobody does except Carol. At least, I mean—Oliver doesn't know.'

She didn't seem to have much control over her tongue. She couldn't say anything subtle or evasive. She just kept on stammering out crude facts.

'I see.' Colin didn't sound specially shocked, and after a moment Erica gathered sufficient courage to say:

'You won't tell him, will you?'

That sounded rather dreadfully crude, too, of course. But he showed no sign of thinking so. He just said gravely:

'Of course not. It's entirely your own business if you wish to make it so.'

There was a pause, and then he added:

'Don't think me very interfering if I ask how—well, how you're managing things. You see, I consider myself sufficiently a friend to have the privilege of worrying about you, and I feel things must be a bit difficult.'

'Oh, no. They're not at all difficult,' Erica assured him eagerly. 'I live with Carol—Miss Shawn, you know. Do you remember her? You met her at—at our wedding.'

'Yes, I remember her very well.'

'Well, we share a flat together. And I work at a children's clinic, and so I can have Bunny with me. Bunny is my son,' she added in explanation. And she saw that something about the way she said that touched him. She wondered a little why.

'I see,' Colin said again. 'And how old is—Bunny?'

'Four and a half months. Would you—would you like to see him?'

Erica couldn't imagine why she had said that, the moment after it was out. But Colin gave her no chance to take it back.

'I should love to see him,' he assured her quickly. 'Are you really going to ask me home now?'

'If—if you like.'

'I do like—very much indeed,' he told her.

'But aren't you going out somewhere to a celebration supper or something?' she said doubtfully. 'I thought people always did after a concert.'

He laughed at that, however.

'Good heavens, no. What do you take me for? A popular tenor?'

Erica smiled a little, too, then. And they said no more until the taxi stopped.

'Is this the place?' Colin had got the address from her.

'Yes.'

They got out and he paid off the taxi, and they went in at the small iron gate that always squeaked however much you oiled it.

She supposed it was rather strange bringing anyone like Colin Lamb into this sort of place, but nothing like so strange as it would have been to have brought Oliver.

She remembered suddenly, for no special reason, that she had practically never invited Oliver into their old flat in her engaged days. But Colin was quite a different proposition.

Carol came out into the hall as soon as she heard Erica's key in the lock.

'Hello. Bunny's been an angel. Not a murmur from him once. Oh——' She stopped as Colin's tall figure came into view.

'I've brought Colin back with me,' Erica explained quite calmly, as though it were what Carol might have expected. 'He wants to see Bunny, and he's frightfully hungry.'

'No, really——' began Colin.

'Which means that he's frightfully hungry and *then* he wants to see Bunny, I suppose,' interrupted Carol with a smile as she shook hands with him. Then she added candidly, 'I thought you said you were not going round backstage, Erica.'

'I didn't,' Erica said quickly, feeling a little guilty somehow. 'I just—I just——'

'We just happened to meet outside the concert hall,' Colin Lamb explained coolly. 'I wanted Erica to come to supper with me, but she refused on the grounds that she had to go home to her baby. Naturally I threw out a broad hint then that I should like to see—er—Bunny. And so here I am.'

'All right,' Carol said. 'You'd better take him to look at Bunny, while I see what there is to eat. I hope you like eggs, Colin, because I have a suspicion you're going to have to face them in one disguise or another.'

'I adore eggs in every form known to man,' he assured

140

her seriously, and Carol went off, laughing.

'Would you like to come and look at him while he's still asleep?' Erica asked rather shyly.

'Yes, please,' he said. And she took him into the little room which was Bunny's own.

Bunny was lying there very contentedly, his round cheeks very pink and those absurd chestnut curls in flat rings all over his little head.

Colin looked at him with a sort of affectionate curiosity that was amusing and rather touching, Erica thought.

'I don't know anything about them, but he looks nice,' he said in a whisper.

And at that Bunny yawned and opened his great dark eyes.

'Oh, lord! did I wake him?' Colin asked guiltily, and when Erica smiled and said, 'Oh, no, it's time for him to wake now, anyway,' he added, quite involuntarily:

'His eyes are exactly like Oliver's.'

'Yes, I know,' Erica said quietly. 'I notice it every time he looks at me.'

Colin didn't say anything to that, but after a moment he exclaimed, 'Aren't you going to pick him up so that I can see him properly?'

Erica laughed a little then and lifted up the baby. He looked with extreme interest at the big stranger. Bunny liked strangers. In his experience they always admired him. And after a moment he smiled at Colin in a friendly way.

'I say, he's bright, isn't he?' Colin said, and then looked faintly foolish at having been betrayed into such enthusiasm.

'Well, of course he's bright,' Carol said from the doorway. 'What did you expect him to be?'

Colin turned with a laugh, and Erica saw that he rather enjoyed Carol's cavalier way of treating him. She supposed it was refreshing after the 'Oh, Mr. Lamb' variety that were inclined to flock round him.

And when he had gone off very willingly to sample the supper Carol had ready for him, Erica wondered just a little if perhaps Bunny had not been the only reason for his accepting her invitation so eagerly. In any case, she lingered with Bunny as long as possible, so that they might have a

141

little time together.

When Erica finally came in again they were sitting companionably on either side of the fire, discussing life in the general and rather flippant way which seemed to suit them both.

Colin stood up as Erica came in and smiled across at her.

'Carol says I can only come again if you give me permission,' he said. 'So will you please put me out of my misery at once?'

'Of course you can come again,' Erica told him at once, but, really, she was wondering a trifle anxiously how things were going to work out. After all, Colin probably saw at any rate something of Oliver from time to time, and, while she didn't want any elaborate deception, she felt nervously that, after to-night, it was much best not to have any connection with him again.

'Well then, suppose we have things quite clear.' That was Carol, with her deadly literalness and common sense. And, while Erica winced slightly, she was not ungrateful too for the frankness of it.

Colin looked a little taken aback, and Erica decided that she had better do her own explaining. She still felt something of the shock of seeing Oliver again—and of seeing him with Dreda—but she was perfectly calm now.

'You see, it's about Oliver,' she said slowly. 'I don't know how much you know——?' She paused, and Colin said:

'Not very much. Only that you separated.'

'Well, it was more really that I—that I left him. He doesn't know where I am and he doesn't know about Bunny. I don't want any special mystery about it, but, on the other hand, I just don't want—to open things up again.'

(Oh, Oliver! sitting there in the concert hall so dear and quiet. A little pale and worn, and, with his hand hidden under the programme. She wished she need only remember him like that. If only she hadn't seen him come out with Dreda afterwards.)

'Yes, I quite understand.' Colin was speaking now, and he was looking at her very kindly. He must have known quite well, of course, what she had seen that evening.

'I don't know if you see Oliver often?'

'No, not very often.'

'He's away in the north most of the time, I suppose,' Carol said indifferently.

For a moment Erica and Colin looked at each other, but neither of them said that Oliver was in London just now.

'Then I don't suppose there'll be any occasion for awkward questions,' Erica said quietly. 'There's no reason why he should think you have seen me. If anything is said—well, I don't ask you to lie about it, only please just tell him as little as possible. And—and don't mention Bunny, *please*.'

Colin looked troubled.

'I won't, of course, if that is what you really want.' He hesitated. 'Only, do you think that's quite the right thing—well, perhaps I should say, the wisest thing—to do? You must forgive me if I seem interfering, but I have known Oliver very many years, you know, and I can't help feeling that if he knew he had a son——'

'He'd want to take him away in case Erica had a little pleasure out of him,' Carol finished tartly.

'No, no, please.' Erica looked distressed. 'It isn't that *at all*. But I'm afraid he might want Bunny. And—and I couldn't bear that.' Her voice quivered.

'Yes, I understand that,' Colin said. 'Please don't distress yourself, Erica. I was only thinking that perhaps—don't you think he might want both of you?'

'No,' Erica said flatly and baldly.

And somehow there didn't seem much to add to the discussion after that.

Later, when Colin had gone and the two girls were alone together, Carol said, just a little diffidently for her:

'I was glad you were so positive about not re-establishing a connection with Oliver. But I wondered a little why.'

There was a short silence. Then Erica said:

'I saw him this evening.'

'Saw him? Where? At the concert? Did you speak to him?'

'Yes, at the concert. No, I didn't speak to him,' Erica

said without much expression. And then, after another pause—'Dreda was playing. That was why he was there.'

'Oh.' Carol looked very serious. 'Perhaps he came more to hear Colin,' she suggested, not because she had any wish to defend Oliver but because she hated to see Erica look like that.

'No.' Erica's voice was almost cold. 'They came out together afterwards.'

Carol was silent, for she could think of nothing at all to say.

'That was how I saw Colin. I was—waiting—at the stage door. I thought Oliver would have gone round to see them both, and that when he came out I should just catch a glimpse of him. I meant to take great care not to be seen, of course. But I needn't have bothered.'

Erica put her face in her hands suddenly.

'Don't, Erica darling.' Carol stroked her hair fondly. 'It isn't any good, you know, and he—he really isn't worth it.'

'It's absurd, but I can't bear to have you say even that,' Erica said in a sad, muffled little voice. 'I know you only do it because you're so fond of me. And when one's fond of a person I suppose it makes one a little blind to other people and their motives.'

'Oh——' Carol made a little face. 'All right, I'll accept the charge of blindness since it comes from you, though I don't really relish doing it.'

'Oh, it's not only you,' Erica assured her with a faint smile. 'I'm just the same about Oliver. And I suppose—I suppose Oliver is just the same about Dreda.'

But Carol refused to swallow that.

'Oh, no, Erica dear, that's too much. I do draw the line at having us all lumped together with *Dreda* thrown in. You must find another explanation for my reactions. And meanwhile, I suggest we both go to bed. We've stayed up most dreadfully late as it is.'

Erica got up at once.

'Yes. It was having Colin home, of course. But I'm glad he came. There's something so nice about him.' And then, as Carol didn't say anything—'You do like him, don't you,

Carol?'

'Oh, yes,' Carol said indifferently, 'I like him all right.'
And then they went to bed.

In the next few weeks, Colin Lamb became a fairly fre-
quent visitor to the flat. He used to bring flowers for Erica
and cigarettes for Carol, and expensive and somewhat un-
suitable toys for Bunny. Quite often he took Carol out,
because Erica nearly always managed to make Bunny an
excuse for being the one to stay at home.

But one evening, when Carol had been out with Colin,
she came in with the cheerful announcement:

'Next Tuesday it's *you* who are going out with Colin, on
a venture into high society.'

'*I?*' Erica said in astonishment. 'What do you mean?'

'He and the others are going to play at some big musical
party given by a Mrs. Smythe-Smythe or something. It's
the sort of thing the social columns describe as "a gathering
of almost Edwardian formality" when what they mean is
"this rotten bunch of snobs." '

'But where do I come in?' Erica wanted to know.

'Well, he can take someone with him—sister or wife or
second cousin, you know, and it's really very interesting. At
least, he says it is. I suppose it's fun to see how celebrities
behave at close quarters.'

'But why shouldn't you go, my dear? I think you'd enjoy
it quite as much as I should,' Erica said.

'No,' Carol was quite positive, 'I can't. There's a dinner
and dance on that evening in connection with our place and
Madame expects us all to go. She's footing the bill, so that
it borders on the insulting if one refuses. I can't get out of
it.'

'But what about Bunny?'

'Really, aren't you a nuisance!' exclaimed Carol. 'You
just sit there being as contrary as possible when I've
arranged this so carefully for you. You know perfectly well
that Mrs. Jones will come down from the upstairs flat quite
willingly and stay here for the evening. He'll be absolutely
all right.'

'Yes, we could do that, of course.' Erica smiled thoughtfully. She had not been out in the evening for a very long

time, and it did sound rather an unusual and exciting occasion. But even then she felt a little guiltily that they ought to manage somehow so that it was Carol who went. And she said as much.

'No, I really can't get out of this other affair, and, anyway, concerts aren't much in my line,' Carol declared. 'Particularly semi-social ones like this. You go and enjoy yourself. And you shall borrow my green Valerie model. It's a good thing we're more or less the same size and shape.'

'But you've only worn it once yourself,' protested Erica. 'You shouldn't start lending it yet.'

'Why not?' Carol wanted to know. And as no argument would prevail with her, it was in the green Valerie model that Erica greeted Colin when he arrived to escort her. He was by now such a friend of the family that it was quite easy to say to him with a laugh:

'As you will observe, I'm wearing borrowed plumes. You've taken out this dress before, but with a different girl inside it.'

'That's the greatest test of friendship there is,' Carol remarked. 'To lend a dress to a friend, when she looks even better in it than you do yourself.'

Colin laughed, but Erica noticed that he glanced half affectionately at Carol, and she thought, well pleased, 'He thinks she looks lovely in everything. And he's quite right, of course. I wonder——'

On the way there, in the taxi, he was rather thoughtful, and presently she said:

'Are you nervous? I mean, do you mind playing at this sort of affair?'

'No, not much.' He smiled. 'A little, you know. All artists are at almost any concert.'

'Yes, I suppose so,' Erica said. And then she wondered if Dreda knew the meaning of the word 'nervous.'

When they arrived at the house, it turned out to be a large and extremely impressive looking place on the north side of the Park. Inside, it was really beautiful, with large, well-proportioned rooms, very wonderfully furnished. The hostess, too, was large and well-proportioned—and very wonderfully dressed. She was extremely pleasant in a slightly vague way, and was so firmly convinced that Erica was Mrs. Lamb that it seemed useless to try to undeceive her. She did compromise once by calling her 'Mrs. Leyme,' but that was the most she achieved.

Erica didn't really mind. It was all rather amusing, and the one or two fellow-artists to whom Colin introduced her were charming.

There were a great number of people there, some of them well known personalities, at whom Erica glanced with a good deal of interest. The whole thing was slightly like a play in which one couldn't quite decide whether one were an actor or just a member of the audience.

'Enjoying it?' Colin glanced down at her amusedly once, as he piloted her through the crowded rooms, introducing her here and there to people who greeted him.

'Yes, of course. It's most exciting and unusual,' Erica said. 'Though I feel a little bit of a fraud.'

'Why?' he wanted to know.

'Oh, just that it's such a very different world, I suppose, and I'm not a bit like all the other people here.'

'Much prettier and more interesting, you mean,' Lamb said firmly.

'No, I don't mean that at all.' Erica laughed a little. 'And I'm sure that isn't what's in the mind of that fearsome old dowager over there who is inspecting us so haughtily.'

Colin didn't even glance in her direction.

'She's probably envying your youth, my dear.'

'Really, Colin, I don't think she would envy anyone who has the bad taste to appear without any jewels. She has such gorgeous ones herself.'

'Not at all,' he assured her. 'It's when you have to wear pearls the size of spring onions to hide the hollows in your neck that you begin to look a little sourly at those who can afford to wear nothing round their necks at all.'

'You're absurd,' Erica told him. 'And you're getting just as bad at back-chat as Carol herself.'

'Um-hm.' Colin smiled reflectively. 'Carol's repartee is very neat and pungent, isn't it?'

And Erica thought again, 'He thinks everything about

Carol is nice. I'm so glad. Darling Carol!'

Later in the evening, when it was nearly time for the concert to begin, Colin had to leave her. But he found her a nice seat first, from which she could see everything she wanted without being very much in the open herself.

And there Erica prepared to spend a pleasant if uneventful hour.

Her attention wandered a little from the scene around her. She wondered how Carol was getting on at her dinner and dance, and she wondered if Bunny had been good and slept on without waking. Even if he did wake, it wouldn't matter very much. Mrs. Jones was quite capable and very fond of him. Only, Erica liked to be here herself when he opened those great eyes of his and gazed enquiringly round.

Funny that a baby and a grown man could somehow contrive to be so much alike. But he and Oliver——

Suddenly Erica's thoughts came back to the present with a violent jerk. And it almost seemed to her that her heart jerked literally too.

For coming across the room towards her at that moment was Oliver himself.

CHAPTER VII

FOR a long moment Erica said nothing—not even his name. She just stared up at him, her eyes wide and very dark.

It was he who spoke at last, and then only quite formally:

'I didn't expect to see you here, Erica. How are you?'

'I'm very—well, thank you.' The words came with difficulty. 'I came with Colin Lamb.'

'Lamb?' Oliver raised his eyebrows slightly. 'Oh, yes. He's playing here to-night, isn't he?'

'Yes.'

He must be thinking her the most hopelessly *gauche* creature, of course, but she could think of nothing else to say.

'May I sit here beside you?'

She couldn't refuse. It was a very natural request for one's husband to make. But as, wordlessly, she made room for him on the settee beside her, she thought:

'What can I do? What can I say? There's nothing left between us—not even words.'

And then she realised that there was to be something of a reprieve. Comparative silence had fallen upon the company. The concert was about to begin.

She scarcely listened to the music at all, and when the concert was over she could not have said whether it had been long or short.

'Now——' Oliver stood up, dark and tall and slightly overwhelming. 'Let's go and find somewhere where we can talk.'

'Talk?' It was the last thing Erica wanted, and she repeated the word with some dismay. 'But I expect—I expect Colin will be looking for me.'

'Then no doubt he will eventually find you—with me,' Oliver said imperturbably. 'But I think you and I must say a little to each other first, Erica, since chance has brought us together again.'

There was no argument against that, of course, and, feeling strangely helpless, she came with him. They found a secluded seat in the corner of the big conservatory, where the air was artificially heated by hot pipes and artificially cooled by a fountain—to the complete satisfaction of their illogical hostess.

Oliver made her sit down and he himself stood beside her. It had always disconcerted her when he did that, and made her feel very much at a disadvantage. And after a moment she said:

'Oliver, won't you sit down too? It—makes me nervous when you will stand over me.'

He looked astonished—even a little shocked—and sat down at once.

'I wish you would tell me what you're doing with yourself, Erica. I don't know whether you regard it as none of my business, but—well, won't you tell me?'

'Yes. It isn't any great mystery. I work at a children's clinic.'

'Do you?' He looked very slightly amused. 'But do you know anything about children?'

That was rather an odd question from Bunny's father, she thought. But she only said:

'One can learn, you know. And in any case, it's mostly clerical work.'

'I see. And, being adaptable, you are already almost indispensable to them, of course?'

'Well——'

'Just as you were to me.' He was smiling very slightly, she knew, but she could not bring herself to look at him even now.

'Was it—was it terribly awkward, Oliver, when I—left?'

'Terribly,' he assured her. 'But since it was the only time you were even remotely inconsiderate, I can scarcely complain.'

'Oh, I shouldn't have thought you would give me such a good character as that,' Erica said soberly. She was thinking even now of one or two occasions when he had certainly not thought her considerate. But perhaps he was not thinking of those times, because he said coolly:

150

'As a secretary you were always perfect, in my estimation.'

'Oh, yes of course—as a secretary.' She looked very grave.

'I'm sorry, Erica,' he sounded unexpectedly contrite for him, 'I wasn't meaning to draw any special distinction. It was just——' He broke off. And then with quite unusual gentleness he took her hand. 'Do I always say the wrong thing to you?'

'Oh, *no*.' It made her want to cry when he spoke like that, and she turned her hand and clasped his fingers nervously.

'But I nearly always manage to hurt you, don't I?'

She shook her head, unable to find any words that would not bring tears as well. And then she said a little huskily:

'It's quite all right. You—didn't hurt me.'

'I'm glad,' he said quietly. 'Because you are such a good child really, and you—you ask so little.'

That, again, was not at all like Oliver, and she scarcely knew whether it hurt or pleased her more.

He said that she asked so little. Well, she had asked for his love—not in so many words—but she *had* asked for it. And it had been too much. It was not for her.

She thought then of his coming out of the stage door with Dreda, driving home with Dreda. And at that she gently, but quite firmly, drew away her hand.

He gave a slight exclamation, and then she did manage to glance at him. He was looking serious and rather troubled, she thought.

'What is it, Oliver?' she asked, and her voice was gentler than she knew.

He didn't answer at once. Then he said with a sigh:

'I wish there were something I could do, something you wanted which I could give you.' That made her want to laugh, though not very happily. 'But I suppose you've worked things out for yourself by now,' he went on slowly, 'and there's nothing I can offer you which you would accept.'

She thought of Dreda again, and said quietly:

'Well, I don't think there is, Oliver.'

151

He frowned, with that characteristic quick impatience.

'I hate the thought of your working like that. It's absurd when you are my wife.'

'I was never really your wife,' Erica said. Then, as she remembered Bunny, that didn't seem quite the most sensible remark to have made. He seemed to think it silly too, because he said curtly:

'Don't be ridiculous, Erica. Of course you were.'

Her nerves were already badly strained, and his impatience had the effect of tightening them disastrously.

'Well, I don't need to be paid money for having lived with you in a distinctly limited sense,' she told him sharply.

There was a stiff and rather dreadful little silence.

'I was trying not to mention—money,' he said coldly, and, glancing at him, she saw how deeply he had flushed.

'Oh, Oliver, I'm so sorry.' She put out her hand quickly on his, and it was, quite instinctively, his gloved hand that she covered.

He didn't say anything, but the colour ebbed again, and she saw him glance with a sort of sulky emotion at her hand resting on his.

It was so exactly the Oliver she knew in some of his dearest moods that she wanted suddenly to smile, and to draw his head down against her. But that, of course, would have been a most embarrassing move from an unwanted wife. So she sat quite still, and at last he said, rather unevenly:

'Why do you put your hand on mine like that?'

She didn't know quite what to answer. Then she just said the literal truth:

'Because I like to.'

'Oh——' He gave a short laugh. Then he slowly raised her hand to his lips and kissed it very lightly.

'It's so extraordinary that you don't mind,' he muttered with that little frown which Carol had always said was bad temper.

'But I never minded,' Erica said gently and very patiently, as though to a child. 'Don't you remember?'

'Remember? Yes, of course I remember,' he said roughly. 'It's the chief thing about you that I do remember.

But I've learnt again since then that other people feel differently.'

Other people! Dreda, of course. But what could she say to him? It was no one's fault but his own if he would measure life by the chilly shallows of Dreda's philosophy.

'I'm sorry, Oliver,' she said quietly. And after that there was silence again between them, until they heard a quick, firm step coming through the conservatory towards them.

A moment later, Colin Lamb stood in front of them.

'Oh, Colin!' Erica's exclamation was as much relief as anything else, and she scarcely noticed the surprise in Oliver's glance.

Colin himself looked a good deal taken aback at this *contretemps*, and he said a little doubtfully:

'I'm sorry, I didn't know you were here to-night, Leyne. Perhaps you would rather——'

'No, it's quite all right,' Erica exclaimed quickly. 'We've just finished our talk.' She realised suddenly that she herself must take the situation in hand at this point.

'Well, actually, it's time we went home.'

'Yes, of course.'

It was then that Oliver interrupted.

'I'm sure Lamb will understand that, in the circumstances, *I* should like to take you home,' he said coolly.

But that was not what Erica wanted at all. The very idea threw her into a panic. She looked quickly and almost imploring at Colin, who was, however, quite equal to the occasion.

'I'm sorry,' he said, very pleasantly, 'but I had the privilege of bringing Erica, and I'm afraid I claim the privilege of taking her home again.'

'Well then, good night, Oliver.' Erica held out her hand.

She saw how astonished he was at having his wishes completely set aside. But he took her hand in his left one.

'Am I not even to know where you're living now?' he said in a low, annoyed voice.

'If you like. I'm living in Chelsea,' she told him.

'That's rather vague, isn't it? Chelsea happens to be quite a big place.'

'Very well then.' She was astonishingly cool now. 'I'm

living in a flat not far from Oakley Street.'

And the next moment she had turned and was walking away, with her arm in Colin's.

He didn't say anything to her. Colin could always be relied on to be tactful. And when she had fetched her evening coat and met him again in the hall, he remarked:

'I've said good-bye to our hostess for you, too. There's no need for us to wait any longer.'

'Thank you.' Erica gave him a grateful look, and they went out to the taxi together.

At first they drove in silence. Then he said:

'I'm sorry. It was careless of me not to remember that possibly Oliver would be at that party. He knows the family quite well, I believe, and it was a very natural place for him to spend the evening if he were in London.'

'It doesn't matter, Colin. Don't worry.' And then: 'He seems to be in London quite often now, doesn't he?'

'Well, I suppose his work brings him here sometimes, you know,' Colin explained carefully.

'Yes, yes. No doubt his work brings him here,' Erica repeated rather sadly. And then there was very little further comment until they reached home.

'Will you come in, Colin? Carol won't be home until later, but there'll be coffee and sandwiches, if you like to come in and wait until she arrives.'

He refused, however, saying that it was impossible to know when Carol would choose to come in, and in any case, it was late enough. Perhaps he guessed that Erica wanted to be alone, and that even his sympathetic presence would be irksome.

So she said good night and went into the flat.

Bunny, it seemed, had been as good as usual, and she listened with a rather absent little smile while Mrs. Jones discoursed on his perfections—Mrs. Jones being one of Bunny's most abject slaves.

But at last even that topic was exhausted, and Erica had thanked Mrs. Jones, and said good night, and closed the door of the flat behind her.

She was alone now, and could go over every detail of that evening in her mind. Very carefully she took off Carol's green dress, which she had put on with such pleasure, and hung it on its hanger again. Then she put on her dressing-gown and went back into the little sitting-room, to wait until Carol should come.

At first she sat there in her usual chair by the fire. But after a while she slipped down on to the rug, put her arms in the seat of the chair, and leaned her cheek on her arms.

It was like this that Carol found her when she came in an hour and a half later.

'Hello, pet! Was the chamber music as bad as all that?' She stood there in the doorway, laughing a little and looking very sparkling and brilliant.

Erica roused herself at once to smile back.

'It was lovely, thank you.' That was not specially accurate, of course, because she had scarcely even heard it. 'I had a very good evening. And you?'

'Oh——' Carol came forward and dropped into a chair, 'not too bad. Quite good food—to which I did full justice because it's fun to see the mannequins toying with a grape-fruit and turning green with envy. And there was good dancing afterwards. Excellent band and excellent floor. But I'm tired now.'

'Meaning that you danced every dance?'

'Well—yes.'

'And were very much admired?'

'We have our small social success,' murmured Carol deprecatingly. And at that Erica laughed and put her head against Carol's knee.

'Nice to see you again, Carol.'

'After the lengthy separation? Yes, I suppose it is.' But, for all her flippancy, Carol put a very gentle hand on Erica's hair. 'How did Society receive you?'

'Oh, very nicely, thanks. Everyone was most kind and it was most exciting seeing—people. Your Colin is a charming escort.'

'*My* Colin?' Carol pulled one of Erica's curls out straight, and let it fly back again. 'He's not mine,' she said, smiling a little.

'Oh, yes he is, Carol dear. And he's nearly good enough for you,' Erica said with an affectionate smile.

'Much too intellectual for my taste,' Carol declared.

'Nonsense!' Erica sat up and spoke with a good deal of energy. 'He's just nicely intelligent. That's all. You'd be splendid together.'

'Look here, have you been indulging in some match-making?' asked Carol sternly.

'No, of course not. Only it's perfectly obvious.'

'What is?'

'Why, that he thinks you're marvellous. He used to be so beautifully indifferent and almost cynical about most things. Now he smiles rather artlessly nearly every time you're mentioned.'

'*How* intelligent,' murmured Carol.

'Oh, Carol——'

Carol laughed.

'He's much more your type than mine, really,' she said.

'My type?' Erica looked astonished. 'Don't be silly. It's not a question of types at all.'

'No?' Carol looked thoughtful. 'But I have thought sometimes that you and he——'

'What?' Erica interrupted her before she could get any further. 'What on earth do you mean?'

'Oh, don't be so shocked. Women do sometimes get over the first bad mistake, you know, and patch things up very happily with someone else.'

'Do you mean——? Oh, you can't really suppose that I and Colin would ever—think of each other like that.'

'Why not? Later on. If you and Oliver get a divorce, I mean,' Carol said.

'Why not?' repeated Erica. Then she laughed suddenly and flung her arms round Carol. 'For three perfectly good reasons, you idiot. Because it's Oliver I love, and it's you Colin loves, and—most important of all—you love Colin yourself.'

'Nonsense,' Carol protested.

'You do, you do!' cried Erica triumphantly. 'And you've been having some ridiculous, quixotic idea that I should need him. Well, I don't, and I never shall. I think he's a dear, and, as I said, almost good enough for you, but that's absolutely all. *Now* will you admit that you love him?'

'Oh, he's not bad,' Carol conceded. 'Perhaps I'll look him over again.'

'I wish you would,' Erica said as she laughed and kissed her. And she thought—'I won't say anything about Oliver, after all. If she gets the idea that I am making myself miserable again, she might have some silly notion about not wanting to leave me.'

So she said nothing at all of the really important thing which had happened to her that evening. But, afterwards, when she was in bed, she lay staring into the darkness, thinking of the way he had looked when he said—'Why do you put your hand on mine like that?'

It was a little difficult to hold to her determination not to mention Oliver, because it was so much easier to tell Carol everything. But this time Erica kept her own counsel.

When Colin next came, she contrived to see him for a moment first, and just said casually—'By the way, I didn't mention to Carol about meeting Oliver the other night. There—there didn't seem to be any special need.'

'No, of course not,' he agreed tactfully, and addressed himself to the simple task of coaxing smiles from Bunny.

Erica supposed, after that, that she might consider the whole incident closed. She was not in the least likely to meet Oliver again casually, and, in a way, the very fact that they had now met and talked things over seemed to have written 'finis' across the page.

Until then, there had always been a vague feeling that he might turn up in dramatic circumstances, that—for good or ill—their paths might cross again.

Well, now they *had* crossed—with remarkably little result. Any questions which he had been asking himself were presumably answered. He could dismiss her from his mind —so far as it was possible to dismiss any woman who had been one's wife.

Evidently it had worried him to some extent to know that she was somewhere in the world, perhaps needing the only thing he was willing to give her—money. Now he had ascertained that she was in no want, and so he need worry no longer.

And, so far as she was concerned, there had been a

successful parrying of any awkward questions. Bunny was still hers, without a breath of a claim from Oliver. She had not even had to dispute the matter. It had simply never arisen.

She ought to feel very thankful and relieved.

And from time to time she told herself that she did.

Once, a little while after the meeting with Oliver, she saw Dreda's name in the newspapers, in connection with some London event. And then she went through the three miserable stages of wondering—Would he come to London for it? Was he here in London now? And had he gone away again yet?

She despised herself for not being able to free herself from this bondage of thought, but nothing seemed to help her. It was not exactly jealousy—at least, she hoped it was not—but a sort of excited unrest that she should almost know about what he was doing and yet be so completely outside his life still.

But there was no help for it. She just had to face the anxiety with what philosophy she could.

The friendship between Carol and Colin was obviously ripening into something else, and in that Erica found a good deal of happiness. For, if she dreaded to think of the loneliness when Carol went, she could find nothing but pleasure in the thought that two people so dear to her should find their happiness together.

His engagements took him abroad for several weeks in the early summer, and Erica rather thought it was that absence which helped Carol to make up her mind.

Certainly, on the day he was due to return, she was quite unusually excited.

'Are you going to meet him this evening?' Erica wanted to know at breakfast-time.

'Well——' Carol thoughtfully flipped the corner of a letter which had just arrived, 'he seems to expect it.'

'Hope it, you mean,' Erica said with a smile. 'I'm sure Colin would never go further than hoping. He's much too gallant.'

Carol laughed.

'Anyway, it seems a pity to disappoint him.'

'Of course. You must go,' Erica decided firmly.

'I'll see what sort of an evening it is,' Carol said.

But, although the evening turned out to be threatening and thundery, Erica was amused and not at all surprised to find that Carol still had every intention of going to meet him.

At the last moment, Erica found that something needed for Bunny had not been sent home from the near-by stores. He himself was safely in bed, and Carol was dressing. So, calling out to Carol that she would be only ten minutes, she flung on a coat and ran out of the flat.

The clouds were already very dark overhead, but if she hurried she could probably get back before the rain actually came. And in any case, there was no time to waste if Carol were to start off in good time.

As Erica came out of the shop again there was a flash of lightning and the rumble of distant thunder. Evidently the storm was coming nearer.

She scarcely realised that there was anyone else in the street at all, until a tall figure stopped beside her. And then Oliver's voice said quite coolly:

'Good evening, Erica.'

She caught her breath in a quick gasp. It was the very last thing she had expected—that Oliver should appear like this. He could scarcely have came there by chance. It must have been intention.

'Why, Oliver,' she said rather helplessly. 'What are you doing here?'

'Trying to find out where you live.' He spoke so imperturbably that she almost thought it must be some form of joke. Except, of course, that jokes were not at all in Oliver's line.

'But how absurd!' She laughed nervously.

'Why? I happened to be in London for a day or two. It's really very natural to like to know where one's wife is.'

She glanced at him then, and wondered if he were deliberately trying to be horrid. But his expression did not suggest that. He looked obstinate—again she thought ridiculously 'as Bunny can'—but rather disarmingly so.

'Well, it's just along this turning here,' she said.

'Does that mean I can come with you?'

'I suppose so, if you really want to.'

'I really do,' he assured her with a slight smile, and fell into step beside her.

As he did so, the first large drops of rain began to fall.

'There's going to be a heavy storm,' Erica thought desperately. 'And there's no taxi or anything near.' She glanced at Oliver's light grey suit. Not much protection in that against the rain which was coming down quite heavily now.

'This is the place.' She stopped at the gate. And as she spoke there was a terrific clap of thunder, and the heavens seemed to open. Instinctively, they both ran for shelter in the doorway.

It was no good. She must just hope that Bunny was asleep and would stay asleep.

'You'd better come in,' she said reluctantly.

'Thank you——' He paused. 'Do you mind very much, Erica?'

She had no time to answer that, because the door opened, and Carol stood there, ready to go out, in a mackintosh and weather hat.

'I must simply fly. Oh——' She stopped as she saw Oliver, and they exchanged a look of almost equal surprise and dislike.

'All right, Carol.' It was Erica who was the calmest of the three. 'You go along. I know you're in a great hurry, so don't stop for anything now.'

Carol glanced at her, saw that perhaps it was just as well she was going out, and, with the briefest nod to Oliver, started off into the rain.

Without a word, Erica led the way into the flat. Oliver stood there looking round with that air of interested curiosity which sat so oddly on him.

'So you're living with Carol again?' he said.

'Yes. Won't you sit down, Oliver?'

'Thanks.' He sat down. 'I thought you must be, of course.'

'Yes.' Erica smiled faintly as she slipped off her coat.

'I'm afraid Carol found it necessary to tell you otherwise once.'

He shrugged.

'The lie was quite obvious,' he said a little disagreeably.

'Well, I'm sorry, but——'

'Was it really necessary to make such a mystery of things, Erica?' he interrupted.

She hesitated.

'Frankly, I just didn't want you to know where I was, that was all. I'm sorry if it developed into an elaborate mystery. It's always difficult to keep these things within sensible limits.'

'Lamb knew,' he said drily.

'Well, yes. But he respected my wish not to tell you.'

'Oh.' Oliver looked slightly taken aback. 'He has known quite a long time?'

'Yes.'

Oliver seemed to consider that. Then he said slowly:

'I suppose Lamb proved a very good friend altogether?'

'Very, very good,' Erica said earnestly, thinking what a difference he had made to their lives during the last few months.

Oliver looked surprised again.

'Then he comes here quite often?'

'Oh, yes.' Erica smiled a little, because, even then, she could not help thinking, 'And he'll be coming a great deal oftener, if I'm not much mistaken.'

There was a silence. Then Oliver said:

'Erica, don't think I'm trying to force your confidence or anything, but are things better for you nowadays? I mean—I know I never managed to make you happy. I should like to think that you're happier now.'

She could see that he felt an uneasy responsibility about her. She supposed that was why he had been so anxious to find her and reassure himself.

'You mustn't worry, Oliver,' she said quietly. 'I have a good deal to make me happy now.' It was true, she told herself fiercely. Bunny was enough to make any woman happy.

161

'I'm very glad.' He smiled slightly. A remote smile—the smile of a stranger, she thought. 'If there's ever anything I can do to—make things easier——'

'Thank you,' she interrupted quickly. 'I—I should tell you if there were anything you could do.'

'I see.'

There was another pause, and Erica thought how terrible this was. This half embarrassed attempt to smooth down the broken edges. She had loved this man so desperately, lived with him, had a child by him. And now they were talking like business acquaintances.

Evidently he felt the constraint, too, because he glanced out of the window, and then said, with obvious relief:

'The rain is stopping now. It was very kind of you to let me come in. I think I'd better go.'

She knew from the jerkiness of the sentences how put out he was, but there was nothing to say. She got to her feet, too, and stood there facing him. Neither of them said anything for a moment. It was difficult to know how to make this good-bye which seemed so final.

And then the silence was suddenly broken—not by either of them, but by a succession of impatient little calls from Bunny's bedroom.

Erica stood there petrified. But Oliver was galvanised into sudden speech.

'What's that?' And then, as the colour was suddenly whipped into his face, '*Who* is that?'

She didn't say anything even then. She just went out of the room and across to Bunny's room.

He was lying there, clutching ineffectually at the bars of his cot, and grumbling to himself. He stopped as soon as he saw her, and smiled engagingly, as though to distract her attention from the fact that he should be asleep.

Erica bent over him. He had kicked off most of the cot clothes, and his curly hair was rubbed up into warm, coppery fluff where he had been rolling about on his pillow.

To his extreme pleasure and astonishment, his mother lifted him up. She turned slowly, the child in her arms, to face Oliver, who had followed her and was standing now in the doorway. For a moment he and Bunny stared at each

162

other with the same great dark eyes. Then he said, almost in a whisper:

'Who is he, Erica?'

'He's Bunny,' Erica said, through rather dry lips. 'Don't you recognise your own son?'

CHAPTER VIII

OLIVER came slowly forward into the room, watched all the while by Erica and Bunny.

'Please give him to me,' he said at last, rather huskily.

Erica gently detached Bunny's clutching fingers from her neck and handed him over. Oliver took him—clumsily because of his injured hand—but very gently. Then he sat down and turned Bunny so that he could look at him.

'Are you—really—my little boy?' he said slowly, and for a moment his perfectly beautiful smile just lifted the corners of his mouth.

Bunny liked the smile, but became suddenly bashful under the continued gaze of those dark eyes. He looked at Erica for reassurance, and when she smiled, he smiled too. It was evidently all right.

His gaze wandered round for something else to distract him during this pleasant variation of his evening routine, and then, very carefully and thoughtfully, he laid his little crumpled hand on the back of Oliver's gloved hand.

His father gave a choked exclamation, and caught him close.

'You're like your mother,' he said, and suddenly covered his face with kisses.

Erica was astonished at this emotional display from Oliver, of all people. But Bunny was more than astonished. He was quite unused to such violence, and didn't approve of it at all. Down went the corners of his mouth.

'No, no, no——' Half laughing, Oliver got up and carried him over to the window. 'You're not to cry. You mustn't be afraid of me. That's like your mother, too. But you mustn't be like her in that.'

'Oliver!' Erica spoke in half shocked, half amused protest. And Oliver smiled at her then over Bunny's head.

'Well, isn't it true?' he said defiantly.

'I suppose so. But haven't you always meant that it

should be so?'

He didn't answer that. He kissed the top of Bunny's head and said, 'His hair is just like yours.'

Erica wanted to ask, 'Then why kiss it? Wouldn't you rather it were like Dreda's?' But of course she did nothing so childish.

She said instead:

'And his eyes are just like yours.'

'Are they? Let me look at them.' He put a finger under Bunny's round chin and tipped up the little face. 'Why, so they are.' He laughed with obvious pleasure, and at that Bunny laughed too.

'How old is he, Erica?'

'Nine months.' Erica stood there divided between pleasure and apprehension at Oliver's delight in the child.

'Nine months?'

'Yes. He was born on the last day of September.' It was strange how, once the salient fact was out, every detail had to be told.

'Nine months,' Oliver said again. 'Oh, Erica, why didn't you tell me? Didn't you think I should be interested?'

'I was—afraid,' Erica got out with difficulty.

'Afraid?' He glanced across at her again. 'Why?'

'That—that you might want him.' It sounded terrible blurted out like that, but what else could she say? The fact had to be put into words some time.

'Oh——' Some of the light went out of Oliver's face, and he smoothed his little son's hair nervously.

'Colin said that perhaps we ought to tell you, but——'

'*Lamb!*' Oliver's face went rather dark. 'Do you mean that Lamb knew all about—my son, while I——'

'I'm sorry, Oliver. It must seem strange——'

'It does.'

The curt interruption stopped her. And then, perhaps because he remembered what she had said about his frightening her, he spoke more gently:

'Well, what did Lamb say?'

'He—he thought perhaps we ought to tell you. But I was afraid you might not let me keep Bunny, and then—and then I think I should just have died.'

Oliver gave her a queer little look.

'I shouldn't have tried to take away your baby, Erica. The law would never let a baby be taken from its mother in these circumstances. Have I really made you think I'm such a beast?'

'No—oh, no!' She was distressed at that. 'Only——'

'Only what?' he asked gently, as she stopped nervously.

'Well, there have been times when nothing in the world would make you change your mind about something. I didn't know—what arguments—I could use, except that I loved him. And my love has never counted for very much in your eyes, has it?'

There was a long silence.

'I'm sorry, Erica,' he said slowly at last. 'I'm sorry and ashamed, for I am afraid there's a lot of suffering behind that sad little speech. And it's suffering that I have caused.'

She wanted to say something reassuring, to start making excuses for him, but, of course, there were no excuses to make, because it was the bitter truth.

'I was just never the man to make you happy, in spite of your touching devotion.' She saw him bite his lip slightly, perhaps because her devotion *had* touched him, even if he had no use for it. 'The fault was all mine,' he went on doggedly, although she knew how much he hated owning himself in the wrong. 'I know that now. It was outrageous of me to marry you, feeling as I did about—someone else.'

'You were quite frank about it,' Erica said in a whisper. 'I had my eyes open.'

'Yes, I know that,' he frowned. 'That sounds very good in theory. But I remember you once called it "an abominable bargain" and you were perfectly right. Everything that happened afterwards came directly from that.'

'You mustn't reproach yourself so much.' Erica came a step nearer in her earnestness. 'You couldn't know that Dreda would come back, or that your—love for her would flame up so fiercely again.'

She saw that he didn't like her even mentioning his love for Dreda, because he drew back and looked rather remote and haughty. Oh, well, she supposed he considered it almost a sacred subject. Some men were like that—and nearly always about some woman as worthless as Dreda.

Oliver dropped his eyes a little sullenly. And then, suddenly, his expression changed.

'Oh, Erica, he's asleep,' he said very softly.

It was quite true. Bunny had long ago lost interest in a scene in which he no longer played star rôle, and now he was fast asleep, one hand still spread out against Oliver in an attempt to grasp a button that was out of reach.

Erica came over, smiling a little.

'Shall I take him?'

'Perhaps you'd better.' But Oliver gave him up reluctantly, she could see, and then stood watching her as she put him back into his cot.

'You need never worry again, Erica,' he said at last. 'He's yours absolutely. I should never attempt to make any sort of claim to him, you know. Please believe that.'

For a moment she felt too deeply moved even to look up at him, and when she did she smiled a little unsteadily.

'Thank you, Oliver. That's very generous of you.'

'Generous?' He laughed rather shortly. 'I don't think our relationship has been marked by my generosity, exactly.'

'You mustn't say that,' she exclaimed. 'You mustn't really, Oliver. There were many times——'

But he stopped her before she could go any further.

'Don't try to whitewash me, Erica,' he said, taking her hand with a slight smile. 'We won't go into the rights and wrongs of it all now, but, believe me, I know where the responsibility rests. Only even the worst of mistakes can be partially undone.'

She wanted to stop him—to do anything to hold back the words which she knew were coming. But he went on slowly:

'You can leave it entirely to me to see that this mistake is undone. And, even if you had a great deal of unhappiness out of your marriage to me, I hope it will seem to you that Bunny was something to set against it on the credit side. That's why I want you to have him—absolutely—as yours.'

'Thank you, Oliver. I—do appreciate what you're doing.'

Oh, God, they were getting back to absurd, stilted speeches again, when all she really wanted to do was to put her arms round his neck and say: 'Dearest, stay with us. See, you already love Bunny. I won't ask that you should love me, too. Only stay with us—stay with us. Please, please, if you have any pity, stay with me.'

But of course she couldn't. She had to look at him stolidly, and say idiotic things about appreciating the fact that she was allowed to keep the son that she herself had borne.

Neither of them said anything for a moment after that. Then he moved to the door, without even looking again at the sleeping Bunny.

'I'll go now.'

He, too, had evidently found the scene a little too much, and was glad to be going.

She followed him into the hall. There was no question this time of their kissing each other good-bye, of course. They had come a long, long way from even that terrible day when she had first left home.

She looked at him and thought: 'He is almost Dreda's husband already. I wish I were dead. Yes—in spite of Bunny—I wish I were dead.'

He looked at her just then, a little embarrassedly.

'You'll be hearing from—from my lawyers, you understand.'

She passed the tip of her tongue over her dry lips.

'Yes, of course. I understand.'

Silence.

'Well, that's really all, isn't it?' she said at last, unable to bear the tension any longer.

'Yes. Except about Bunny'—he spoke rather rapidly in case she should take fright—'I mean, I'd like to make some arrangement about money for him——'

'It will not be necessary,' she said very coldly. Very ridiculously, too, she knew, for perhaps it was scarcely fair to refuse so much on Bunny's behalf. But she thought, with fierce hurt pride, that if he preferred to let them both go for the sake of a woman like Dreda—well, they would stand on their own feet.

She didn't want Bunny to be supported by Dreda's husband.

'Do you feel very strongly about that?' He looked troubled.

'Yes, very. Neither Bunny nor I need anything from you.' She was sorry it sounded so ungracious, but there it was. These things had to be said occasionally.

'Very well.'

He made no more protest. He hesitated briefly, then slightly nodded to her like a stranger. She opened the door for him, and watched him as he fumbled for a moment with the latch of the gate. She felt the old familiar impulse to run to his assistance, and then the old familiar flash of tact which had always prevented her from making such a mistake.

Then he went out of the gate and along the road. Presently he turned the corner. And that was the end.

Erica closed the door and went back into the dining-room. The air was still hot and thundery, but she was shivering uncontrollably.

After a while she began to cry. There was no one to stop her. Carol would not be in for hours. Bunny was asleep. Oliver was gone. She could cry and cry as much as she liked. And perhaps by and by her heart would not feel so exactly as thought it had been broken in two.

Sometimes she used to look back on that evening afterwards and think that perhaps it had been the low water-mark of her despair. She never knew how long she wept. Only, after what seemed like hours, she found that she was crouching on the rug in her old, characteristic attitude of grief, her arms in the seat of a chair, and her head on her arms. Her eyelids felt stiff and heavy, and it seemed as thought she had shed all the tears that could ever be shed.

She looked at the clock, and realised that Carol might be home at any time now. She must not be found like that— not on any account. Besides, possibly Carol would bring back Colin with her, and it would be too awful that they should both find her like this.

Erica dragged herself to her feet, and went to wash the tear-stains from her face. And when Carol came in—alone —just after eleven, Erica was looking very calm, and even managed a perfectly natural smile.

Obviously relieved, Carol asked, without any preamble:
'What happened, Erica? Is everything all right?'

'Oh, yes, everything is quite all right,' Erica assured her, while she thought that it was really a very extraordinary way to describe what had happened that evening.

Carol took off her coat and sat down.

'I was never so astonished in my life as when I opened the door and saw him standing there with you. Where on earth did he *come* from? I didn't know whether I was deserting you by going, or really being super tactful. But I gathered that you preferred to deal with him alone.'

'Oh, yes, you were quite right to go.' It was so dreary having to go over it all again, but, of course, Carol wanted to know what had happened. 'He just—happened to be somewhere near here, I suppose, and I ran into him. He—he walked along with me—seemed rather interested to know where I was living now. And then when the rain came down so heavily I couldn't do anything but ask him in.'

'I'd have let him drown first,' muttered Carol, but Erica took no notice, and after a moment Carol asked rather sharply, 'Did you manage to keep him in ignorance about Bunny?'

'No.'

'*No?* What happened?'

Erica didn't answer at once. She seemed to be living over again the moments when Bunny's voice had sounded so imperiously, and Oliver's face had changed in that extraordinary way.

'Bunny—called out,' she said at last. 'And of course Oliver wanted to know who it was.'

'And you told him?'

'What else could I do?'

'Was he—did he like him?' Carol asked with irrepressible curiosity.

Erica bit her lip hard and nodded. She was thinking of the way Oliver had caught up Bunny and kissed him over and over again. Then she changed the subject.

'Carol, was it a specially nice evening?'

'Yes, I think I'd call it that,' Carol admitted indifferently.

'Don't be so tiresome. Tell me at once what happened.'

Carol came and put her arm round Erica.

'It seems hateful to tell you this evening, of all evenings,' she said, 'but yes, we are engaged.'

'Oh, my dear,' Erica kissed her very tenderly, 'I'm so glad. I'm so really glad. Nothing could have been nicer.'

And she thought, 'Carol too has gone. I wouldn't have it otherwise for the world, but Carol, too, has gone. I have lost her. Only Bunny is still with me.'

But nothing of that must reach Carol herself. She must only know how truly glad and happy Erica was that this delightful thing should have happened.

'When are you going to be married, Carol? And are you terribly happy?'

'Fairly soon and—yes,' Carol said laconically.

Erica laughed.

'You'll make him a splendid wife,' she said affectionately.

'I hope he'll make me a splendid husband,' Carol said grimly. 'That's much more important, to my way of thinking.'

Erica didn't say anything to that, partly because she thought Carol was not entirely serious, partly because her own theories had not proved so overwhelmingly successful. But for quite a long while they sat up talking together, and when they finally went to bed, Erica was looking much less white and strained.

She let Carol go on ahead and went into Bunny's room for a moment, as she always did, just to see that he was all right. He was lying there fast asleep and very comfortable, quite unaware that he had been the centre of a tense scene that evening.

Erica hung over him for a moment, feeling a certain comfort in him, as she so often did.

'Oh, darling, I'm so glad he loved you,' she said softly. 'Even if it hurt him a little too, I'm glad, because in a way you're part of me. And he did kiss you when he said you were like me. At least he did do that.'

And with that very small piece of comfort to hug to her heart, Erica kissed her little boy and went quietly to bed.

During the next few days there was quite a lot of excitement about Carol's engagement. They saw a good deal of Colin, who was the perfect picture of the man who had found his own happiness, and the few people they knew seemed quite touchingly pleased to hear of Carol's happiness.

'I think everyone has been extremely kind and interested about it,' Erica told Carol.

'And I think Bunny's the only one who's kept his head at all in all this excitement. You shall be my page, darling, if you can stagger in time.'

Carol picked him out of his cot and held him up admiringly. Usually he laughed delightedly, as soon as she did that. But this time he just flicked his thick, dark lashes at her and refused to smile.

'What's the matter, my sweet? Is your Auntie Carol's form of humour beginning to pall? Or do you just disapprove of her marriage on principle?'

'I think he's feeling the heat, Carol.' Erica came over to look at him too. 'He's been very quiet indeed to-day. Do you think he looks all right?'

'Oh, yes.' Carol refused to take it too seriously. 'He's just arriving at a graver stage of his philosophy. Aren't you, Bunny?'

'Maybe.' Erica smiled a little, but she gave her baby rather an anxious little hug as she took him from Carol. 'I'll get Dr. Sallent to look him over to-morrow if he's still so quiet. He is usually so full of beans that it seems unnatural to have him like this.'

'He'll be all right, you'll see,' Carol said consolingly.

But when the morning came Bunny was not all right. He was hot and restless, and very much inclined to cry. It was such an extraordinary state of affairs with the even-tempered Bunny that Erica sent a message to the clinic to say she could not come that day, and then telephoned for Dr. Sallent.

She knew it was nothing at all serious, she kept on telling herself. There were a thousand things that could make a baby cross and feverish. But so many things had slipped from her desperately clutching fingers in the last year, that

172

she had an almost superstitious horror of anything happening to Bunny.

Dr. Sallent arrived before she could indulge in any more wild imaginings, however, and his calm manner steadied her at once.

He stayed quite a long time with Bunny, examining him very thoroughly, and never once did his cool, self-reliant manner vary.

'Well?' Erica said at the end, and anxiety had put an edge to her usually soft voice.

'I don't want to make grave statements in a hurry, Mrs. Leyne, and I don't want you to start frightening yourself unnecessarily, but I should like to call in a colleague of mine for a consultation.'

Erica stared at him in wordless dismay.

A consultation! That meant something serious. When doctors began to consult, it meant that parents had to sit by, sick with anxiety, hoping against hope that one of them— one of them would be able to say what was the matter and what should be done.

'You have no objection, of course?'

She realised then that she had not found words to answer Dr. Sallent.

'Do whatever you think right,' she said in a whisper.

'Now, please——' Dr. Sallent patted her shoulder very kindly. 'Please don't start getting into a panic. Your little boy is going to be perfectly all right, but we're not taking any chances.'

'No—no, please don't take any chances.'

He didn't understand, of course. He couldn't possibly know how her nerve had been broken long ago. She had seen her happiness filched away, bit by bit, so that now it took practically nothing to terrify her.

Probably all Bunny had was a simple, childish ailment. But she couldn't make herself believe it. Not if she repeated it to herself a hundred times. Instead, her broken nerves kept on pushing her into the dark places, when she could only pray over and over again:

'Not my baby, God. Everything else has gone, but please not my baby, too. I'll be good. I'll never complain again.

173

Only let me keep Bunny.'

And, of course, it was all so silly because there was nothing seriously the matter with Bunny. Dr. Sallent had said not.

At least, Dr. Sallent had *almost* said not.

But Dr. Sallent said something quite different when he and his colleague had examined Bunny again that afternoon. He made Erica go out of the room while he and the other doctor spoke together. And then Dr. Sallent came out to her by himself.

She only needed to look at his face once. She knew then quite well that her fears had not been silly at all.

'It's serious, isn't it?' she said despairingly.

'Yes, I'm sorry, my dear, but it's very serious. It would be wrong to pretend anything else. It's a case for an operation, and a pretty quick one. Within twenty-four hours at any rate.'

I must get Oliver. Her husband—and Bunny's father. That was the only coherent thought in Erica's head just then.

She didn't know exactly when the doctor left. Something seemed to be wrong with the dialling arrangements, and she was finally forced to obtain help from an operator. But, in the little pause before a voice said, 'Here is your Northmead number coming through,' she realised that she was alone.

Then Oliver's voice said clearly and calmly:

'Yes? Leyne speaking. Who is it?'

'Oh, Oliver, is that really you? It's Erica.'

'Erica! What is it? Is something wrong?' Even all that distance away she could hear the concern in his voice, and it warmed her frozen heart.

'Yes. It's Bunny. He's very ill. He has to have an operation. Oliver, you must come, you must!'

'I'll be with you early in the morning. And don't cry so, child, don't cry so. You'll make yourself ill.'

It was only then she realised that she was crying, and to have Oliver speaking comforting words to her, all the way from their own home, made her want to cry harder than

174

ever. But she managed to choke back her tears, because he was speaking to her again.

'I'll drive down the motorway, Erica, and be with you as soon as ever I can. Keep up your courage, my dear. There's not much the doctors can't do nowadays. Who is the surgeon? Do you know?'

'Yes.' She was calm again by now. 'Sir James Price, I think the doctor said.'

'Oh, he's a splendid man. We couldn't have a better. He'll pull our little boy through all right.'

'Thank you, Oliver. Thank you for being so kind.'

He didn't say anything to that, but returned her 'good night' rather gently before he rang off.

There was not very much sleep for Erica that night. Bunny was taken away, very late, to the nursing home, and she was told that the operation would be the following morning.

'Oh, yes. My husband will be here by then,' she said earnestly, and felt there was some comfort in being able to say that.

Erica never forgot that meeting with Oliver in the grey early hours of the morning. He came straight from the station to the flat, and his first words to her were:

'Thank you, Erica, for letting me come.'

There was such strange humility in that for Oliver that it touched her beyond expression, and as he came into the little hall, she slipped her arm into his.

She felt him press her hand against his side, in the intimacy of an anxiety shared, and she said:

'I'm so glad to see you, Oliver. So unspeakably glad.'

Then Carol came out and greeted him with curt kindness, and presently she persuaded them both to have some breakfast.

There was really not much said between the three of them. Oliver asked some sharp question from time to time, and Erica—and occasionally Carol—gave him the replies. There was only one subject they wanted to speak of, and very soon the pitifully little that could be said about it became exhausted.

About half-past nine Dr. Sallent fetched them in his car

to the nursing home. He was not aggressively cheerful, only perfectly calm and collected, and he patiently went over the ground again with Oliver.

'You seem to know Bunny and his state of health very well,' Oliver said once.

'Well,' Dr. Sallent smiled slightly, 'I brought him into the world, and have kept an eye on him since then. He's a wonderfully healthy baby and has a pretty fair chance of weathering this.'

'Yes, yes. It's just that one gets abnormally anxious about—about anything so small.'

For a moment Oliver looked so exactly the anxious father that Erica glanced at Dr. Sallent, wondering what he was thinking. She saw that the doctor could not altogether hide his surprise, and presently he said a little drily:

'I'm glad Mrs. Leyne has you with her. As you say, the anxiety is specially acute in the case of a small child, and she has had to manage one or two difficult things on her own in the past.'

Oliver didn't say anything to that. He looked very faintly haughty. Then he glanced at Erica, and his expression changed. She didn't know quite why, but he put out his arm and drew her gently against him.

'All right, Erica, you're not alone now,' he said in a very low voice, so that even the doctor could not hear. And for a moment she pressed her face against him and thought: 'It's going to be all right. It *must* be all right when Oliver is as kind as this.'

At the nursing home, too, everyone was very kind to her. They let her and Oliver wait in a bright, pleasant room that was not at all like the usual waiting-room. No big, dusty table or faded leather chairs or grisly comic papers. Just a pleasant sitting-room with a chintz-covered sofa and chairs, and a big bowl of flowers on the table.

Sir James Price came to see them for a moment or two before the operation. An extraordinarily handsome man with strong, beautiful hands and unusually light grey eyes, he gave Erica a feeling of confidence at once, and she thought:

'I don't mind trusting Bunny to him.'

He didn't say anything sentimental about Bunny. Just explained that the case was an unusual one, but by no means a hopeless one, and, if it were humanly possible, he would give their little son back safely to them. It was always terrible for those who had to wait, but would they try to keep up their courage, and he hoped there would be good news for them soon.

'I've never known Mrs. Leyne to be anything but brave,' Dr. Sallent said. Then they both went away, and she and Oliver were left alone together.

'I think that's quite true,' Oliver said after a moment's silence. 'I've never known you to be anything but brave either.'

'Oh, Oliver'—she smiled very faintly—'I'm afraid I'm really inclined to be a coward. At least, I often feel dreadfully frightened about things.'

'That isn't the same thing at all. Come and sit down here on the sofa, Erica. You can't have had much rest last night.'

'No. It's—it's difficult to rest, isn't it?' she said rather pathetically. And at that he took her hand in his and held it very firmly.

She had no idea how long they sat there in silence. And then he spoke again.

'I can't tell you how grateful I was to you for letting me come,' he said gently.

'I had to ask you. I needed you—and you're his father. I really think you love him—don't you?'

'Yes.' He spoke softly. 'That's what made it so hard to give him up to you so completely, and face the fact that another man would bring up my son.'

She stirred sharply in his arms.

'Another—what? What do you mean?'

He bit his lip a little, and she saw he had gone pale.

'Well, when you marry Lamb, I suppose——'

'I?' Erica exclaimed in stupefaction. '*I'm* not going to marry Colin Lamb. Carol is.'

'But you said——' He broke off suddenly, and, to Erica's unspeakable horror, she saw his mouth tremble.

'Oliver!' She put up her arms round his neck, and, for

the first time, without any thought of fear, she kissed him over and over again on his lips, until they were steady enough to respond.

'Darling, what are you doing?' he said rather huskily at last.

She remembered Dreda then. But Dreda seemed to have shrunk to an infinitesimal degree of importance.

'I'm—kissing you,' Erica said, with a little smile. 'Do you like it?'

He bent his head then and gave her a hard, firm kiss on her mouth.

'Yes, I like it,' he said curtly. 'How about you?'

'You know the answer to that,' she told him rather shyly. 'You always have.'

'Have I? I seem to have been making a few fool mistakes just lately. Do you really mean you're not going to marry Colin Lamb?'

'Why, of course I'm not. How could you possibly think it?'

'Well, he was for ever hanging round you,' Oliver said grimly. 'And you told me what a very, very good friend he was, and he seemed to know far more about Bunny than I was ever allowed to know.'

'Oh, Oliver, I'm so sorry,' she whispered. 'I just—happened to meet him one night, and I blurted out about Bunny, and he wanted to come home and see him. I wasn't very keen really, but in the end I let him come, and almost at once I saw that it was not so much Bunny as Carol that he had come to see. He was terribly taken with her even at our wedding.'

'Was he?' Oliver said in great astonishment. 'I didn't notice.'

'Well, no, nor did I at the time. Only I realised it afterwards.'

'And you say it's Carol he wants?'

'Yes.'

'You're sure of it?'

'Why, of course. They're engaged.'

'Oh, God, how wonderful!' He held her close suddenly and kissed her.

'Oliver, I don't understand,' she said a little timidly.

'No, dear, I don't see how you could——' he began.

Then he broke off. Both of them had suddenly gone rigid, and their eyes met in a sort of desperate attempt at courage.

At the end of the passage there was a slight stir, and the sound of footsteps approaching. Everything had been so quiet before that there was something almost menacing in the breaking of the silence.

'Oliver, I'm so afraid,' she whispered. 'I'm so terribly afraid.'

'All right, my dear,' he said calmingly. 'You have me.'

Erica stared at him, her eyes full of a strange relief, for with those words he seemed suddenly to have broken some hideous spell. She had been telling herself for so long that she had no one but Bunny, no one but Bunny. It had frightened her that all her happiness should be wrapped up in one person, as though tempting fate to take everything away at one blow.

Now that was changed—utterly.

'You have me,' Oliver had said, and it was true. By some inexplicable, glorious miracle she *had* Oliver. Perhaps he would tell her how, some time, but at present it was enough that she could cling to him and know he was hers.

She was still clinging to him when the door opened, and Sir James came in, followed by Dr. Sallent. The specialist was smiling slightly, as he stood there thoughtfully turning down the long fingers of one hand with the other.

'Well, that's another very nice little life saved,' he said kindly.

And then Erica fainted.

CHAPTER IX

WHEN she came slowly to the surface again, she could hear voices saying something about, 'Oh, yes, yes, the strain, you know.' 'Considerable anxiety.' 'Not specially strong anyway.'

But the voice she wanted to hear was not there.

She lay there not daring to open her eyes. He was not there, of course. It had all been a dream. There was something about Bunny, but he was all right. He was safe. And she had thought Oliver was there. But that had been wrong.

She felt the tears gathering slowly behind her eyelids, and presently, in spite of all her efforts, they forced their way under her lashes. She was very much ashamed to be crying like this, but the disappointment was so bitter.

'Erica, my dear,' his voice said very quietly. 'What's the matter?'

She did open her eyes then, to stare up at him through her tears.

'What is it?' he repeated gently. And she stammered:

'I—I thought you'd gone.'

'Gone? You couldn't think I would leave you just now, child?'

'No. I just thought you hadn't been there, after all. I've dreamt it so often before, you know,' she explained rather sadly. 'And I—I always woke up.'

'I see.' He bit his lip again. 'Well, it wasn't a dream this time. I'm really with you—and I'm staying with you.'

'Always?' she whispered. But he had turned to speak to Dr. Sallent, who had come over just then, so he missed that timid little query.

'Hello.' Dr. Sallent smiled at her as he took her wrist. 'Feeling better now?'

'Yes, thank you. I'm sorry to have been so silly.'

'No, no, nothing of the sort,' the doctor told her. 'It's been a nasty strain for you.'

'I am afraid my unpardonable weakness for the dramatic had something to do with it too,' said Sir James's deep, pleasant voice, and Erica turned her head to see that he was still standing by the window, talking to a slightly self-important-looking nurse.

'Oh, no,' Erica smiled at him, 'it wasn't that at all. However you had put it I think I should have—have fainted with relief.'

'Well, don't go fainting any more,' he told her. 'It is my pleasant privilege to hold the centre of the stage, once the patient is removed. You rather stole my thunder, you know.' But he smiled so kindly that she knew it was all right.

'Sir James,' she held out her hand to him, and the great surgeon came over at once and took it, 'I can't thank you, you know. I can't possibly thank you. There—there are no words.'

'That's all right, Mrs. Leyne. It's my job, you know. Just as producing nice children like—what is it?—Bunny, is your job. We both do our jobs very well, I think. Here's to our mutual admiration.' And he bent his head and kissed her hand very charmingly.

After that, he went off with the self-important nurse, who looked faintly disapproving by now, but not at all surprised, so probably Sir James always made nice little speeches like this.

Erica looked after them, smiling slightly. Then her eyes came back to Dr. Sallent, who smiled too.

'I like him,' Erica said. 'Quite apart from his having saved Bunny's life, I like him. I think he's nice.'

'Oh, yes,' Dr. Sallent agreed, with a touch of amusement. 'He's usually considered very charming as well as clever.'

'A little bit too much like a middle-aged stage hero,' remarked Oliver drily. Whereat Dr. Sallent laughed outright.

'Perhaps. But when you can perform the miracles that Sir James can, you're entitled to a few minor vanities, I suppose.'

'Very likely,' Oliver agreed with a grim smile.

'And now, Mrs. Leyne, I think I'll just run you and your husband home, and you shall get some rest. You can't have had much last night.'

'But Bunny——' Erica started up on her elbow. 'I want to see Bunny.'

'Oh, no, no, no.' Dr. Sallent shook his head with a smile. 'I'm afraid there isn't any question of your seeing him until late this afternoon, or this evening. I promise you that you shall be phoned as soon as it is possible to see him, but there is plenty of time to rest first.'

And with that Erica had to be satisfied.

It was not until she reached home that she realised to the full how weary she was. And then she could scarcely do more than reassure Carol as to Bunny's safety, and fall into bed, and sleep and sleep.

It was later afternoon when she woke, and Oliver was sitting there in the room quite near her bed. He was not reading or anything. Just gazing away thoughtfully out of the window, and, although his face looked worn, it was exceedingly tranquil.

'Oliver,' she said softly.

He turned to her at once, and leant forward to put his arm over her.

'What, my dear?'

'What were you thinking about just now?'

'Um?' He touched her cheek lightly with his lips before he replied. 'I was realising, for the first time in my life, what an exceedingly fortunate man I am—and how very little I deserve it.'

'Oh, Oliver——' She put up her hand and patted his cheek. 'How absurd. Why shouldn't you deserve good fortune? You're very good and sweet yourself.'

He laughed, rather unhappily.

'How can you, you dear little idiot? How can you possibly say that to me, after the way I treated you—the odious things I've said? Could you ever forgive me?'

'Oh—I think forgiveness is an absurd word,' Erica said.

'Do you? I had rather hoped to hear it from you,' he confessed.

'But what does it mean, really? If a person isn't sorry,

182

there's nothing to say. And if he is—well, no one in the world can be *more* than sorry, and I think real contrition wipes out the fault.'

Oliver laughed softly.

'It's a very merciful creed, Erica. Thank God it's the one by which I'm to be judged.'

'I'm not judging you at all, Oliver,' she said gently.

'No? Don't you want to say anything hard to me?'

'Of course not.' She smiled a little. 'But I do want to ask you a question.'

'Well, you have an excellent opportunity.' But Oliver's smile had a touch of anxiety.

'Oliver, what made you change your mind about—about Dreda? For I think you must have changed it very much.'

'You did, first of all,' he told her. 'And then'—his face hardened—'and then Dreda did.'

'Oh——' Erica looked very serious. 'When—when did it happen, Oliver?'

He put his head down against her suddenly.

'The day I came home and found your letter.'

'*Then?* Oh, but it couldn't have been as early as that.' She stroked his hair with rather agitated fingers, and she noticed, as she had that night at the concert, how much the grey in it had increased.

'Why not, Erica? No, don't stop stroking my hair. Please go on. It makes me realise why Bunny looks at you the way he does.'

'What—did you say? Oh, Oliver, *you* once looked at me the way Bunny does,' she said, and her voice trembled.

'I did, dear?' He lay so that he could look up at her, but his cheek was still against her. 'When, in heaven's name, did I look like Bunny?'

'When we were in Verona,' she said a little timidly. 'That night when——'

'Oh, God, yes—I remember now.' He turned his face against her then, and kissed her where he lay. 'Of course I looked as Bunny does. I suppose I felt as Bunny does,' came in a muffled voice.

'What do you mean?' She smiled, but her lips were very unsteady. 'What do you mean, Oliver?'

183

'I mean, darling, I probably knew in that moment that you were everything which mattered. Peace and safety and contentment and happiness. Only, being a fool, I forgot it once more, and you see I had to learn it all over again from the bitterest experience. But Bunny is a wise child. He knew it once and for always. That's the difference between your husband and your son. Bunny has something of you in him, and so he's much wiser and dearer than I shall ever be.'

'To me you'll always be the dearest thing in the world,' Erica said simply. 'Whether you want it or not, it will always be so.'

'I do want it,' he said with equal simplicity. 'And I always shall. I want it so that I'm afraid of the very thought of your turning away from me.'

'You need never be afraid about that,' she told him gently. 'Now tell me about Dreda.'

He stirred uneasily against her. And then he said impulsively and childishly:

'I hate Dreda.'

Erica laughed. She couldn't help it.

'You baby,' she said, and drew him close against her. 'Was she very horrid about something?'

'About everything,' Oliver whispered, and gave a long sigh of content because he was with Erica and not Dreda. 'But of course, if I hadn't been such an utter fool, I should have known what to expect long before. It started that week-end—you know—when I would go to London. I didn't really want to go much in the end. It was a sort of idiotic gesture of self-assertion. I suppose I didn't make myself specially pleasant——'

'I expect you were simply frightful. Poor Dreda,' Erica said tolerantly.

'Oh, don't.' He moved against her again, and then laughed a little. 'You think I'm a fool, don't you?'

'Yes, a bit,' Erica said, but she kissed him, and that took the sting out of what she was saying.

'Well'—he frowned—'I was punished, anyway. It was a hideous week-end. Disillusionment and self-disgust the whole time. And then, all the way home, I was really thinking thankfully of you. I tried to imagine ways of telling you

184

how sorry I was, but of course they didn't come very easily to me in those days.'

'He imagines they do now,' thought Erica amusedly. 'Oh, Oliver! I'm glad you're not really much changed.'

'And then when I got home, you were gone. There was only your letter.'

'Poor darling, I'm so sorry.'

'No, I'm not,' he said slowly. 'I've hated every bit of this miserable lesson, but I wouldn't have been without it, Erica. I—have learnt just a few things.' He gave her a look of half sulky humility, and she could not bear that he should abase himself any more.

'Hush, my dear. I've learned some things too——'

'You?' he interrupted. 'You had nothing to learn. You were everything that was sweet and good already.'

'Oh, no.' She laughed a little at that. And then, as a sudden memory struck her: 'But you did see Dreda one other time, didn't you?'

'Yes. How did you know? It was after that that I really hated her.'

Erica's eyes opened until they looked simply enormous.

'Tell me,' was all she said in not much more than a whisper.

'I'd really gone to hear Lamb, you know,' Oliver said slowly. 'And, partly, I think, just to show myself how utterly dead my feelings for Dreda were. Afterwards I went round back-stage to see Lamb.'

'Yes, I know.'

'You *know*? How?' He looked up quickly.

'I was there—at the concert.'

'Oh, my darling,' he said gently, 'were you really? How strange. I was thinking of you nearly all the evening.'

'And I was looking at you nearly all the evening,' she told him. 'But never mind. Please go on.'

'She was there, of course, and—oh, I suppose she wanted to show her power over me. She insisted on my taking her out to supper afterwards. I dare say I wasn't very gracious about being forced into it.'

'I'm sure you weren't,' murmured Erica, but he only smiled faintly at the interruption.

'And she turned to me suddenly, with all those back-stage people round, and—asked me to fasten her bracelet. I had—to use—both hands, of course.' He had gone rather pale at the memory of it, Erica saw. 'She knew quite well what it meant to me, and while I—struggled with the damned thing in front of them all, I really just wanted to put my hands round her throat and choke her.'

And she had supposed he was absolutely absorbed in Dreda when he had come out that night!

'Oh, Oliver, I'm so sorry, darling.' She could feel that he was trembling slightly, just as he had that time before when he had spoken about his hand. 'Don't. You're all right now.'

'Yes, yes, I know. Of course it's all right now,' he said a little feverishly. 'It always is when I'm with you. And it's the same with Bunny. He doesn't mind either. He put his hand on mine at once. That's why I loved him so much. I thought then that if I could have stayed with you both it would have been heaven. But I imagined you wanted to marry Lamb, and it seemed to me that I was being given just a chance to do one decent thing for you at last.'

'And *that* was why you said you were going to divorce me, and—and that I could have Bunny?'

'Yes.'

'But you would have had nothing at all then.'

'I didn't deserve anything, Erica,' he said quietly. 'I know that now.'

'My dearest——' Erica was unspeakably touched. 'And all the time you really wanted him?'

'I wanted you both—terribly. But you most of all.'

She kissed him then, very softly.

'You know you have us both, for always, don't you?'

'Yes.' Then, after a long silence: 'You know that I'll try to deserve you, don't you?'

She didn't protest about it. She just said: 'Yes, Oliver.' And after that, he lay against her for a long while, 'looking as Bunny did.'

He was still there when Carol knocked on the door.

'Erica, are you awake?'

'Yes?' Anxiety had suddenly come back into Erica's heart.

'You're wanted on the telephone, dear—from the nursing home.'

'I'm coming—oh, I'm coming!'

There was such hope and fear in the cry that Carol winced. And when Erica had run to snatch up the receiver her eyes met Oliver's for a second.

'It will be all right. They were perfectly confident this morning,' Oliver said mechanically.

'Yes, I know. But she's lost her nerve a little where the people she loves are concerned.'

Again their eyes met, and just for a moment Oliver's fell.

'I—understand.' He spoke slowly and with a good deal of difficulty because his pride was not quite so humbled as he had thought it was.

'I hope you do,' Carol said drily.

Oliver looked at her with lively dislike. And then suddenly, because she had loved Erica and been good to her when he himself had failed her, he swallowed the last remnant of his pride.

'You needn't be afraid for her again,' he said with extraordinary gentleness. 'I have learnt my lesson.'

'I'm very glad.' Carol's voice was rather more gentle, too. 'Because, you know, she is entirely at your mercy.'

'Oh——' Oliver looked a little horrified. 'Need you put it like that?'

'I think so,' Carol told him grimly.

And then Erica came flying back to them, her eyes shining and a dash of excited pink in her cheeks.

'It's all right. He's going on splendidly. We can see him. Oliver, we can see him!'

And suddenly she was in her husband's arms, weeping tears of passionate relief. And Oliver was comforting her in a way that made Carol raise her eyebrows a little, and then go away in search of Colin, because she saw she was no longer needed there.

Later, when Erica and Oliver were setting off for the nursing home, Carol drew her aside for a moment, just to kiss her and whisper, 'Is everything in the world all right now?'

'Everything, Carol dear.' And Erica's smile said very much more than the three words could.

It was true. Everything was all right. She had Oliver beside her and she was going to see Bunny, who was safe. There was nothing else in the world that she could ask.

Dr. Sallent met them at the nursing home, and took them in himself to where Bunny was lying, very still and quiet, in his little white cot. And as they stood either side of him, watching for him to open his eyes, Erica thought:

'How wonderful it is to share your baby with your husband. Ten thousand times better than having him all to yourself.'

They were silent, all three of them, for quite a while. Then Oliver said quietly:

'How like you he is, Erica. I'm so glad.'

She looked across at him quickly and smiled.

'Do you think so? I always think he's just like you. And I am glad it should be that way.'

'Well, of course, of course,' Dr. Sallent said. 'He's the image of both of you. All really tactful babies are.'

They all laughed a little then. And at that moment Bunny opened his great dark eyes, and smiled very faintly too, because, in point of fact, the little joke belonged to him by right.

Other titles available this month in the Mills & Boon Classics Series

3 specially chosen re-issues of the best in Romantic Fiction

BY FOUNTAINS WILD
by Anne Hampson

"What is there in marriage for a woman? I wouldn't marry the best man breathing!" declared Kim. But she was as wrong as are most girls who make this rash statement!

CHATEAU OF FLOWERS
by Margaret Rome

Fleur had married Alain because she loved him — not, as he thought, either because he was blind and she felt sorry for him, or because he was rich and her motives were completely mercenary. But how could she ever convince him of the truth?

BLAZE OF SILK
by Margaret Way

More than anything else in the world Dana wanted to clear her father of the scandal that so unfairly hung over his name. How annoying that the only person, apparently, who could help her do it was that infuriating Brett Cantrell!

Mills & Boon Classics

— all that's great in Romantic Reading!

Available November 1978 — 50p each

DON'T MISS NOVEMBER'S
GREAT DOCTOR - NURSE ROMANCES

CHRISTMAS AT ST. PETER'S *by Jane Andrews*
The night of the Christmas dance at St. Peter's is
the most romantic date in the hospital's calendar.
But for the staff who have to stay on duty, like
hard-working theatre sister, Jo Henderson, and her
adored colleague, Dr. Laurence Harvey, even missing
the dance can lead to something very special . . .

EMERGENCY FOR DR. BILL *by Peta Cameron*
(This Starry Stranger)
It takes a plane crash to show Peg MacPhee, air
hostess, and Mrs. Lucia Anello, the only other sur-
vivor, that there is a gentle side to the surly Dr. Bill
Ransome. Delivering Lucia's baby before their rescue
forges a link between Peg and Bill which is almost
severed by jealousy and suspicion.